Chilopodophobia

Chilopodophobia

Paul McMahon

A

Grinning Skull Press

Publication

PO Box 67, Bridgewater, MA 02324

DEDICATION

This one is dedicated to my Mom, Charlotte McMahon, who read me every book in the house when I was young, and then got me a library card when I'd memorized them all by age 5.

CONTENTS

Acknowledgments

This one developed over a number of years, inspired and encouraged by a number of people. Mr. Caputo, who assigned his Home Economics class a project to create an advertising campaign for a new product, as well as members of my first writing group: John D. Harvey, Jack Haringa, Don D'Ammassa, Lon Prater, and Paul Tremblay.

Special thanks to my latest writers group, who saw this one all the way to the end: Trisha Wooldridge, Susanne Lahna, Catherine Grant, and Laura J. Hickman.

CADY, THEN

1

The sight of the family mansion as they rounded the driveway failed to take Cady's breath the way Ezzy promised. Maybe because they'd arrived late and the sun had dropped beneath the horizon, causing color and clarity to melt and run. The size of the place was impressive, and it benefited from the climbing driveway, which forced his perspective upward, giving its Tudor-style jagged roofline awe-inspiring height, but it fell short of his idea of a mansion by at least a handful of rooms.

As they approached the garage, Ezzy driving extra slow to give him time to gawk, the house stretched to the right like a lazing giant. The front door, arched and sporting long decorative hinges, stood above two stairs, matching bronze sconces on each side. To the door's right, behind short shrubs, a pair of curtained windows glowed with interior lights. On the door's left, between it and the garage, rose a stone castle turret. According to Ezzy, the turret housed a spiral staircase that led to her bedroom. She'd warned him his own room would likely be on the opposite side of the house, across from Uncle Fritch's rooms.

Cady hadn't met a girlfriend's family in a very long time. It had to mean good things to be invited. Some of the evening would pass as expected, from the first utterance of "I've heard so much about you," to the inevitable "Take care of my niece if you know what's good for you," speech. Having lived seven years resigned to spending the rest of his life haunted by memories of Priscilla, Cady would take any threat of vengeance Ezzy's uncle dished out with grace and gratitude.

"I told you it was impressive," Ezzy said.

"You were right. It's breathtaking."

Ezzy squeezed his thigh, causing a quick tremble down his leg, making him gasp. She laughed. "I'll stop. Uncle won't be happy if we get too familiar around him."

"I'm going to miss being familiar with you, then."

"I know you will." Her eyes shone green in the light over the garage door. Cady's heart seemed to melt into a cloud of bliss. The intensity of the moment made him feel unanchored, unattached to reality. It was a little like when he'd been drinking, only there was no anger to weigh him down. Love really did make you feel like you could fly.

Ezzy leaned toward him as if for a kiss, but at the last moment she snagged her purse from the back seat and straightened up. She glanced at him, twitching her head around to fling her soft black hair out of her face, and smiled. "Do you want something?"

"You have no idea."

"I'm pretty sure I've got an idea." She leaned over and opened her mouth to him, her tongue soft and quick, her lips lingering. "I'm gonna need the key," she said as she pulled away.

"The key?"

"It's in the cup holder."

"Oh." Cady took a slow breath, watching her as she pulled a black box out of her purse. She pressed a button, and the garage door in front of them started to growl as it pulled up.

Cady found the cup holder between their seats and stuck his fingers inside. He didn't feel anything. He slid sideways and looked inside, saw the gold-colored key resting at the bottom. He looked up as he reached for it again, expecting to see the white stonewall or naked studs of a normal garage, but he saw trees, instead.

"Wow."

He rubbed his fingers together and realized he'd missed the key. He looked again. It still rested in the exact same place. He hadn't even felt it.

"What the hell?"

Ezzy laughed.

"Did you—" He turned on his overhead light and peered into the cup holder. The key rested exactly where it had been. His fingers hadn't even knocked it aside. "You *painted* this?"

Still laughing, Ezzy pulled a keychain out of her

purse by a gold-colored key.

He looked at the painted key again. Ezzy's incredible three-dimensional detail work fooled him again, and he stuck his fingers inside, even knowing the key wasn't really there. "You have an amazing t—"

He almost choked as the car pulled into the garage, giving him the full forest glade effect painted on the walls.

"You did all this?"

The wall to the left of the car showed a copse of trees, complete with a brook running along in the background. A distant hill rose above it, speckled with blue flowers, while unmoving birds, chickadees, gold-finches, and nuthatches, perched on closer branches. A good-sized Ford pickup sat in the next bin, obscuring the artwork on the right wall. Rising in front of them, looking alien in the field, stood a short staircase and a wooden door with a bronze knob.

"Damn, Ezzy. You are one talented—"

The door pulled open. A large, barrel-chested man stepped out. He wore black chinos and a white button down shirt. Uncle Fritch. Ezzy hit the button on her little black box, and the garage door started growling down.

"Let's go say 'hi,'" Ezzy said.

Cady took a deep breath as he climbed out of the car. The garage roof had been painted to look like a calm blue sky, with a "V" of birds far up, heading off to who-knows-where.

"Hello, dear," Uncle Fritch boomed. The man's voice would make the average drill instructor crumple with envy. "It's good to see you again."

He'd felt a little sorry for Ezzy when she'd told him Uncle Fritch was her only living relative, but now he found the information comforting. It meant he only needed to impress one person tonight. There wouldn't be any inter-familial politics to watch for, and Ezzy had already alerted him to the subjects (religion and capital punishment were the biggest) to steer away from. So unlike Pris's family…but he'd thought about her enough for tonight. No more.

Cady lingered by the car, giving Ezzy time to hug her uncle and step into the house.

"Hi," Cady said. He extended his hand, having to reach up as Uncle Fritch moved to the top of the stairs to look down at him. The move was deliberate, Cady was sure, intended to intimidate. Cady kept his discomfort off his face, though. He kept his smile on and his hand outstretched while Uncle Fritch sized him up.

The man's hair was curly and cropped close to his head. A thin beard stretched down to cross his chin like a strap, while a skinny mustache rested along his top lip, independent of the beard. It was an odd look on such a large man. Made it seem like he'd outgrown his own hair.

"Hello, Cady," Uncle Fritch said, seizing his hand in a strong grip. "I've heard a lot about you."

"All good, I hope."

"From Ezzy, all good is what I've come to expect."

2

Cady entered the house when Uncle Fritch gestured him through the door. Ezzy waited for him at the end of a short hallway. He walked after her, hurrying as she turned right. A doorway to the kitchen stood on the left after he took the turn; he caught a glimpse of an older woman in an apron cooking something that smelled terrific. Ezzy walked past, then took another right. Cady followed and stepped into a large foyer.

He bit his tongue before he could say a word. The wallpaper in here was a dark maroon with an ugly black swirl pattern that swallowed the light. He kept walking, noting the large staircase leading to the second floor and the smallish door beneath it, probably leading to a cellar. He saw a crack in the wall running from the cellar door to the skirt board, and one of the balusters was missing halfway up. The carpet here was dark red and frayed in places along the wall, the woodwork darkly stained. A huge chandelier caught his attention. Only a few candle flame-shaped bulbs shone. Even if every one of the dozens of light bulbs was lit, Cady thought it would still be gloomy in here.

Ezzy turned left through a doorway. Cady glanced behind him for Uncle Fritch, but he must have gone into the kitchen. He recognized the inside of the front door, mostly because the stone turret stood beside it. The decorative hinges weren't present on this side. A small, arched opening in the turret revealed the start of the spiral staircase Ezzy had told him about.

He walked after her and entered an average-looking study, dark wood and deep red leathers, maroon curtains and brass fittings. A small home bar stood on the left side of the room, but books were lined up on top, where there should be bottles. On the right, the twin windows he'd seen from outside. In front of them sat a worn green couch, its color out of place, angled away from the window and out into the room. Behind it, a tall reading lamp spotlighted the end of the couch. A medical journal was tented on a pillow. Uncle Fritch must have been reading when they'd pulled in.

"This is it," Ezzy said, turning around and leaning against the huge fireplace on the far wall. "Home sweet home."

"Impressive inside and out," Cady said.

"I thought you'd like it."

He took a step toward her, wanting to embrace her

just once more before they slipped under Uncle Fritch's more prudish rule, but before he got close, the man cleared his throat from the doorway behind him.

"Ezzy," Fritch said. "Grace is getting dinner ready. Would you be so kind?"

"Of course, Uncle."

Ezzy brushed Cady's shoulder as she headed back the way they'd come. He watched her go, then spotted Fritch watching him, probably convinced he was staring at her ass. He forced a smile for the old man.

"This'll give us a little time to talk man-to-man," Uncle Fritch said. He glanced into the foyer, then scurried to the bar and reached underneath it. Before Cady could announce that he didn't drink, Uncle Fritch lifted a clear pitcher filled with something pink to the bar.

"Ezzy told me you don't drink," he said. "So I mixed this old family recipe up just for you. It's iced tea sweetened with watermelon. Sounds like a kid's drink, I know, but I guarantee you've never had anything like it."

"Sure, I'll try it," he said. Uncle Fritch dumped ice in a highball glass and then filled it with pink. He pushed Cady's drink across the bar, then dumped two ice cubes into another rocks glass and turned to the bookshelf behind him. "Ezzy's a militant teetotaler," he said. He slid a thick volume of poetry aside and pulled out a bottle of Dewar's Scratched Cask Scotch Whiskey. He splashed two fingers into the glass, downed it, and then poured one finger in its place.

Cady closed his mouth and swallowed.

Fritch tucked the bottle away and replaced the book

in front of it. "Between you and me, okay?"

Cady nodded and saluted with his glass of watermelon tea. He rested on the arm of the green sofa. The way it was angled made him want to shove it back against the wall. A quick glance revealed substantial water damage to the window behind it. What he could see of the wall was badly discolored, too.

Fritch settled into the large leather rocking chair across the coffee table from him. He took a deep swallow of his Scotch Whiskey, shut his eyes for a few seconds, and sighed.

Cady sulked at his glass of pink tea.

"Ezzy's told me not to lead with subjects that get my dander up," he said. "Doesn't leave us much to talk about, so I guess it's up to you."

He leveled his gaze directly at Cady and waited. Cady took a slow breath and sipped his drink. The sweetness hit him hard, cloying in its intensity. He swallowed and managed to keep most of the reaction off his face. "This is pretty good, once you get past the sweet," he said.

"It was Ezzy's favorite growing up."

Cady swirled his drink, surprised there were no bits of fruit in it. He took another sip, and this time, prepared for the onslaught, he liked it even more.

"So what do you do with yourself, Cady," Uncle Fritch asked.

"Between jobs, currently, the economy trashed as it is."

Fritch smiled. "The state of the economy is one of

those things Ezzy won't let me talk about." The man took a slow swig, as if to rinse away his opinions, then returned his attention to Cady. "What would you be doing if the economy hadn't left you jobless?"

"Retail work, I suppose. Salesman-type stuff. Not that I'm very good at it."

Fritch creased his brow. "If you're not good at it, why would you choose it?"

"It's easy to do, and it brings in enough money to get by so I can concentrate on my real work, which is playwriting."

Fritch's eyebrows went up. "Playwriting? Unusual. Most people would just say 'writing' and leave it at that."

Cady nodded. "I've done that in the past, but the word encompasses so much it's always followed by the question 'What kind of writing?' which drags a conversation out."

"You don't like long conversations?"

Cady shrugged. "A playwright will live or die by the strength of his dialogue. How could I convince you I was any good if my answer prompted a usual or predictable response?"

Fritch thought for a moment. "What am I going to say next?"

"You're going to ask me if I've written anything you've heard of."

"Exactly what I was thinking."

"I've haven't had anything produced, yet, no."

"Interesting phrasing," Fritch said.

Cady took another sip of his drink. If he wasn't careful, Fritch could start asking about his past, which would not do at all.

"Are you close to your family? Do they live around here?"

"Not especially. I betrayed their expectation that I follow in the family business."

"What business?"

Cady swallowed. Was it his imagination, or was something squiggling beneath Uncle Fritch's collar?

"Furniture," Cady said. "Unfinished."

Fritch downed the last of his drink and stood. He wandered behind the bar again, pausing to run a finger along the spine of the poetry book, and then dumped his ice into the sink with a *clunk*. He reached under the bar and stood with a can of diet soda.

"You shunned your family's retail business so you could work in other people's retail shops?"

"Thus, the nature of their annoyance with me."

Cady downed his own drink and stepped toward the bar. Kid's drink or not, he'd acclimated quickly. His mouth watered while Fritch refilled his glass. When he took it back, it was all he could do not to gulp it down like a man wandering out of the desert.

"Ah, Grace," Fritch said.

Cady turned to see the older woman from the kitchen standing in the doorway. She wrung her hands together just beneath her breasts. Her skin was so pale her hands almost disappeared in front of her white apron.

"Pardon, sir," she said. "Dinner is served."

"Beautiful," Uncle Fritch said. He poured his soda into a glass, then gestured to Cady's drink. "Refill?"

Cady gaped at the empty glass in his hand. It had just been full. When had he done that? In a daze, he handed the glass to Uncle Fritch. His gaze locked onto the edge of the big man's collar. He could have sworn something moved under there.

3

Cady's stomach gave a loud grumble as he entered the dining room. Ezzy grinned at him, but Fritch either ignored it or didn't hear. Fritch sat at the head of the table, while Cady and Ezzy sat on each side. Conversation lagged while they ate. Twice, his feet found Ezzy's under the table, but with both of them wearing shoes it wasn't as intimate a touch as he wanted. Still, her smile elicited delicious memories of the night before.

Cady surprised himself again by finishing another tall glass of watermelon tea. As soon his glass touched the table, Grace entered the dining room and placed the pitcher of pink tea in front of Uncle Fritch. He, in turn, refilled Cady's glass.

"If I keep this up," he joked, "I'm going to drown in my teepee."

Uncle Fritch groaned, Ezzy just shook her head.

"Do you use puns like that in your work?" Uncle Fritch asked.

Something in Fritch's tone caught Cady's attention. He looked at the man, saw his collar move the slightest bit, and realized he was hearing a faint buzzing sound. As if someone very far away was mowing grass. Maybe his ears were ringing.

"I never use puns in my work," Cady said.

Fritch nodded. "Good. Puns are the devil's play-things."

Cady stared at him.

"Uncle, are we going to have to add puns to the list of things you're not allowed to talk about?"

A smile crossed the big man's face. "Just putting your friend on, my dear." He finished his soda and contemplated the empty glass for a moment. He sighed as he placed it on the table. "Just out of curiosity, Cady, what kind of plays do you write?"

"Drama, mostly. Some mysteries."

"Murder mysteries?"

"Um…well, yes." Something was clearly off now. Aside from the buzzing, which he tried hard to ignore, Fritch seemed irked about something.

"How do they turn out, your murder mysteries?"

Cady looked at Ezzy. She was watching him calmly but seemed ready to bust out laughing. Were they having him on about something?

"I'm not sure what you mean."

"I mean the play, dear boy. How do your murder mysteries turn out?"

"The murderer is discovered, of course. Arrested."

"Arrested, but not brought to justice?"

"Justice? No. The story ends with the arrest."

"You realize that by ending it there, you let the audience assume justice will be served."

"Um...yes. If all the clues point the same—"

There. The corner of Uncle Fritch's collar twitched. Both his hands rested on the table, so he couldn't be playing a trick on him. Something was definitely under his shirt collar.

"But even with conclusive evidence," Fritch was saying, "murderers get off all the time. Technicalities and such rubbish."

Cady met the man's eyes. Did he know something? Had he been digging into Cady's background? He spoke carefully. "Some of those who get off on technicalities are actually innocent."

"So the money-grubbing lawyers would have us believe."

Cady nodded. "Okay." He didn't know what else to say. The conversation had veered too far out of his comfort zone.

"So you're okay with the murderers in your plays going free?"

"Um..."

"Uncle," Ezzy said. "You're getting awfully close to discussing the prison system. You promised you wouldn't."

A few seconds of uncomfortable silence passed, and then Uncle Fritch smiled and placed his meaty hand over hers. "You're right, my dear. My apologies." He turned to Cady. "No harm, no foul." The hint of a smile played across his face.

Cady nodded, feeling more dazed than ever. Something brown and slender dropped down from beneath Fritch's collar, bent in the middle, and then darted out of sight. "It's okay," he made himself say. He closed his eyes and moved them away from the big man, opening them again to see Ezzy, who was grinning at him. Her expression might have been inquiring after his health, or it might be anticipating whatever was coming next. Cady shrugged in response.

Watermelon tea my ass.

He snuck the glass to his nose and sniffed it. Nothing out of the ordinary. He brought it to his lips, intending to taste whatever drug Fritch was using, but couldn't stop himself from downing the whole thing. Good stuff, that.

Uncle Fritch cleared his throat. "Ezzy, God bless her, never told me how you two met."

Cady swallowed. "Not all that inn'esting."

"Sure it is. I'd like to hear the story."

Cady sighed. He looked at the man, prepared to start the story, but the centipede resting on his shoulder stopped his thoughts cold.

"I caught him stalking me outside the post office," Ezzy said.

Cady jolted at her words. "No. Thass noddit. Not. It."

"What was it, then?" Fritch asked.

Cady shut his eyes and took a slow, steadying breath. They had to know he was intoxicated. Fritch must have spiked the tea with something. Powerful shit. Had Ezzy said he worked as a pharmacist?

Just hold on a little longer, he thought. He peeked at Uncle Fritch.

Centipedes swarmed on his clothes. They crowded on his shoulders, their many legs wriggling for position and traction. One of them had grown so large its head was the size of one of the roasted potatoes he'd just eaten. He saw where its eyes met in the middle of its face, watched its mandibles stretch apart and click together. He was imagining this. Had to be. Hallucinating. The large centipede cocked its head to the side as if to ask if he was sure.

"Cady? If you weren't stalking her, then what were you doing? How do you explain your actions?"

Two centipedes dropped to the table and started toward him on wriggling legs. "I was a kid," Cady said. "Woods. Rotted nest. I fell. It ran across my cheek. Tangled up in my hair."

Ezzy let out a low whistle.

A tear trickled down his cheek. "I don't want to be a kid. I don't want them on me. Please."

The first centipede lifted its head up onto the edge of his plate. He wouldn't have thought something with an exoskeleton could alter its expression, but this thing looked angry.

"Could you tell us about... Priscilla," Fritch asked.

The second centipede skirted around his fork and

sank its mandibles into Cady's little finger. He jerked away, but the chair grabbed his ankles and twisted him to the floor. There were more centipedes down here. They rushed at him. The pale green rug swirled with intricate black lines, all of them squirming, squiggling, chomping to sink their mandibles in his flesh and devour him with a million minuscule bites.

Cady tried to keep his face up and out of their reach, but he was so tired. Suddenly so tired.

From above the table, Fritch's voice. "You do remember Priscilla, don't you, Cady?"

TRILLING

4

"The knives, they nip."

Cady heard the voice, realized he'd been hearing it for a while.

"The knives, they bite."

He opened his eyes the slightest bit. He saw the bars and knew what this place was.

"The knives they chew and chew and chew."

Cady sucked as much air into his lungs as he could.

"But me, I sit."

He moved his hand, felt the bare mattress someone had placed him on.

"And me, I wait."

He tried to push himself into a sitting position but his brain processed only pain, so he dropped back down.

"And me I'll never, ever win."

He waited, listening to the voice recite its poem

again. On the last word, Cady mustered every ounce of his strength and shoved himself into a sitting position. He managed to swing his legs off the cot and catch himself, elbows on knees, before he flopped to the floor. He concentrated on his breathing, and eventually, his spinning vision coalesced and solidified.

He raised his head. The bars stood almost in front of his face. Another prison cell stood across the hall, just as narrow. Within it, a fat little man sat cross-legged on the floor in the lotus position. The lighting sucked, a single dim bulb, low to the ground. Its shadows made it impossible to discern the fat man's facial features, but Cady could feel the man watching him.

"Where are we?" Cady asked.

"End of the line. Edge of the knife. No one off. No one off."

"Lovely."

"The knives, they nip."

"Yeah, I got that, thanks."

"The knives, they bite. The knives they chew, and chew, and chew."

"How long have I been here?"

The man finished his ditty. "Not long enough. A while. Not long enough."

Cady took a deep breath. "HELLO!"

"No! Don't make him come! Don't make him come! He brings the knives!"

"Who? Who brings the knives?"

"The Grandpa Man."

"The Grandpa Man," Cady echoed.

"He brings the knives."

"I'll bet he does."

Cady placed his hands on his knees. It took a lot more strength than he expected, but he managed to stand. Gritting his teeth, he leaned forward against the bars.

"Hello?" he called. "Anyone out there? I want a lawyer. Tell me what I'm being charged with or let me out!"

He waited.

"You're going to make the knife man come," the other prisoner said.

"That's what I want," Cady told him. "HELLO!"

"No. No knives. No more."

Cady watched the man put his head down and mewl into his arms. He took a moment to study his surroundings.

The cells were mirror images of each other, floors of poured concrete, ceilings and three walls made of stone, front walls made of metal bars. The bars ran floor to ceiling, inches apart, and were held in place by three evenly spaced horizontal slats secured to the stone walls on each side. Both cells contained a metal cot with a single bare mattress, as well as a five-gallon bucket in the corner. He didn't wonder at the purpose of the bucket. The outhouse reek in here was terrible. The other man must have used his already. If they thought Cady would be shitting in there, they had another think coming.

"Hey out there! I want my lawyer! I want my phone call!"

"The knives, they nip. The knives, they bite."

Cady waited, listened to the man recite his mantra, which was how the man needed to deal with his situation. Unfortunately, Cady would only be able to take so much of it. On the fourth recitation, Cady started snapping his fingers at the man.

"Hey! Hey, you!"

The man left off in between lines.

"What's your name?"

"Trilling."

Fitting, Cady thought. "Where are we?"

"Where?"

"Yeah. Where? What prison is this?"

Trilling gestured around him. "We are prisoners of the Grandpa Man."

Cady sighed. "Okay, I'll bite," he said. "Who's 'The Grandpa Man'?"

"I'm afraid he means me," a deep voice boomed to Cady's left. He turned his head to see Uncle Fritch standing a few feet beyond reach, shrouded in shadow. He had changed from his white button-down to a light blue polo, but a dozen or so centipedes still clung to his barrel chest. Every one of them gazed at Cady.

5

Cady took a moment to ensure his first sound wouldn't be a scream. He gathered his thoughts and did his best to ignore the vile creatures on Fritch's shirt. When his mind tossed up a picture of Ezzy, though, the anger overran his control.

"Where is she?"

"She?"

"Ezzy! What have you done with her?"

Fritch watched him for a few moments. "I assure you, she's not the one in danger. In fact, when I left her, she was locked in her room. Back at the family home, I mean, pining for you."

Cady blinked. "Pining?"

"Yes. After you collapsed at our dinner table, very rude of you, by the way, I had you taken by ambulance to a nearby hospital." He used air quotes. "You 'slipped into a coma.' She believes you've been transported to

Washington."

"What?"

"Poor Ezzy was crushed to learn your family wasn't as estranged as you let on. They paid for your transport across the country. Those bastards didn't even let her say goodbye."

"You son of a bitch."

"The knives, the knives, be careful of the knives!"

"*Can it*, Trilling." He glared at Fritch. "You're not going to get away with this."

Fritch smiled. He took a step toward Cady's cell and bent over, keeping his eyes on Cady. He placed a tall glass of pink on the floor just outside the bars.

"Get away with what?"

Two centipedes dropped to the floor and scurried around in circles before darting between the bars into Cady's cell. He cried out and backed away, bumped the backs of his knees against the edge of the cot, and dropped down to slam his head against the rock wall.

He rolled sideways, curling up on the bed while Fritch talked in a monotone. Cady had the impression the man's words were important, but he couldn't concentrate on them, couldn't understand. It dawned on him that the cells had no doors. He wanted to ask Fritch about that, but unconsciousness toyed with him, stealing his ability to speak.

Trilling was babbling now. "I confess… I confess… I confess…"

Fritch kept talking to Cady. "Do you know what you need to do?"

What? Cady thought. *What do I need to do?*

Oblivion finally washed over him. The last thing he saw was the two centipedes, big around as mice, watching him from the hall.

6

Cady woke on the floor, his body stiff as stone. Every movement tore through joints, twanged ligaments. His neck wouldn't turn; his spine was straight and insisting it stay that way. His elbow and hip throbbed in time with his heartbeat. He waited, gathering energy. The deep, crooked shadows of the bars scored the walls like retreating claw marks, and yet light glared in his eyes at the same time. How could *that* be?

Cady gritted his teeth while he made small, repetitive movements, working to limber up enough to sit. He remembered the centipedes and snapped his head toward the hallway before he was ready. His neck gave a series of brittle snaps, and his skull seemed to expand like a balloon, but the centipedes were gone.

He put his head back, and the pain of an aggravated

bruise almost made him cry out. He managed to keep quiet, however. Trilling had fallen silent. Maybe asleep. The last thing Cady wanted was for him to wake up and start chanting again.

Cady started the long, slow process of climbing to his feet. He bore every bolt of pain silently. He used the bars to pull himself to his knees and stayed there for a while. He'd passed out on the cot. Some time after, he'd dropped to the cement floor.

Just outside the bars, the glass of pink waited for him. His stomach growled. He fell to his hands and crawled toward it.

He expected plastic but discovered real glass. It fit between the bars with little room to spare. Cady tried to sip it, tried to make it last, but the instant the first drop hit his tongue, he chugged the whole thing. The drink's energy coursed through him like the first blast of water from a showerhead. Moments after sliding the empty glass back into the hallway, he reached up and seized the bars. It took less exertion than he expected to pull himself to his feet.

The bars moved.

It was just a minuscule shift but enough to shove aside the pain in his joints. The glass of pink combined with this small taste of hope charged him with energy. He leaned against the bars, then pulled back with all his weight, but he couldn't tell if they moved again. He tried a few more times with no success. With a determined grin, he locked his fists beneath the middle crossbar. Exhaling, he bent his knees. Slowly, he raised himself back up and tried to lift the bars as he did. They didn't move, and within seconds he needed to lean against them and wait for his head to stop spinning and the muscles in his lower back to unclench.

After a while, he opened his eyes and looked around.

The strange light came from a single, unshaded bulb screwed into what looked like a table lamp. The lamp had been placed on the floor at the head of the corridor, precisely between the cells. The crooked shadows it threw were meant to screw with his equilibrium. He tried to see beyond the lamp and couldn't. It looked like a short, black wall stood behind it, preventing the light from revealing anything beyond.

When Fritch had come in here—Yesterday? Earlier today?—he'd gotten the impression the area beyond the cells was some kind of workroom.

Cady tried to slide the bars left, then right. Nothing, but he refused to believe he'd imagined it. These bars had moved.

"I killed her, you know."

Trilling's voice came from the dark.

"Cut her up."

Cady's chest tightened. Priscilla's face came to him. Fritch had spoken her name. Before.

Cady shuffled backward and sank to the cot. His breathing was shallow and rapid. His blood pulsed through his head.

It had been an accident. An accident. Cady hadn't killed anyone. Didn't matter if they'd been arguing. Didn't matter if he'd downed most of a six-pack before they'd gotten in the car. The accident had nothing to do with his drinking, no matter what the breathalyzer said. Poor conditions. Freezing rain. He'd lost control of the car. Anybody could have. He swerved, overcorrected, and caught the end of a guardrail head-on going seventy.

"The knives, they nip. The knives, they bite."

The metal guardrail had sliced up into his car like an ax blade, cutting through Priscilla easily as if she was part of the upholstery.

"The knives, they chew, and chew, and chew."

"Trilling," Cady said.

"But me, I sit…"

"Trilling!"

He stopped chanting but didn't respond.

"It wasn't your fault, was it?"

Silence.

"The girl you killed?"

"Julie."

"Julie," Cady agreed.

"I killed her. I did it."

"Why aren't you in prison?"

"Mister Lawyer. Mean Mister Lawyer. Technicalities. Unlawful search. Police brutality."

Cady swallowed hard. "Your case was thrown out?"

"I killed her."

"Huh."

"Grandpa Man wants justice served."

"It's not *your* fault. Even if you did kill Julie, the fact that the police screwed up the case is not *your* fault."

"The Grandpa Man wants justice."

Cady rubbed the pain in his back. He expected Trilling to start chanting again, but he heard nothing for a long while. Then he heard the man counting, followed by a sharp intake of breath. He listened but heard nothing as crooked shadows on the walls began to grow hundreds of spindly, wriggling legs.

Cady eased back onto his cot. The cramp in his back twanged once but quieted. He closed his eyes and tried not to think about yards-long centipedes crawling out of the shadows and climbing on top of him, gnawing on his joints.

THE GRANDPA MAN

7

In the dream, Trilling was being eaten by a monster.

Cady opened his eyes to blinding brightness. Far too much light for a table lamp on the floor. There was enough light in here to grow vegetables. There was also enough light to see what Trilling had done to himself.

Cady remembered hearing Trilling count, but that was part of a dream. Wasn't it?

The weird, little man had gotten his hands on a knife. How? Didn't know. He'd dug furrows in his left forearm. Deep ones. Then he'd gone to work on his belly.

Dotted lines of blood had spattered across the corridor, a few of them crossing the bars into Cady's domain. Gross. How do you wash blood off cement?

Maybe the centipedes would eat it. Was blood part of a centipede's diet? It seemed so. Tons of them swarmed Trilling's body, gobbling him up.

Uncle Fritch stepped into the corridor. At least, his barrel chest did. His face was malformed. A crumpled, fleshy scar split it from crown to chin. His eyes were black and glinted in the light. Where his nose should be, two long, flesh-colored appendages stood out to each side, like a costume mustache, segmented like fingers, or tentacles, or…antennae. They were called antennae.

Cady slapped his hand over his mouth. He slid his eyes shut as the creature's horrid face turned toward him. Held his breath until it felt like his lungs would split. Exhaled all at once, then took another deep breath.

The Grandpa Man's true form.

Cady cracked open his eyes. The thing wasn't looking at him any longer. It had wandered into Trilling's cell.

Its clothes were tattered with dozens of little tears up and down the sides. From each tear protruded a pointy, segmented leg, folding and unfolding, like a pugilist prepping to do battle by flexing his fingers.

The Grandpa Man stood over the bloody corpse. The centipedes teeming on it paid him no attention. They entered and exited Trilling's body, using his mouth, his nose, and the bloody gashes he'd made himself. The 'pedes crawled in, the 'pedes crawled out. What came next… Pinochle?

"What a mess," the Grandpa Man said.

Two fat centipedes pushed out of the bloody wreck of Trilling's stomach. They skittered to the floor and approached Cady's cell in a drunken, meandering path, their legs pumping in rhythm like a hundred fingers drumming on a tabletop.

They slalomed around the bars of his cell, back and forth, climbing over each other whenever they met. First one, then the other, stopped to feast on the bloodstains inside the bars.

Darkness swirled through Cady's thoughts, became a whirlpool, a black hole. None of this could be happening, except he was seeing it.

He let the darkness draw him away.

EZZY

8

Cady woke to dimness and crooked shadows again. He lay still for a long time, watching the angled lines on the walls for wriggling legs. In time, he judged himself safe and eased onto his side.

Trilling's cell stood empty.

Not just empty, but barless. Open.

He couldn't see a single bloodstain, either. The faint odor of bleach tinged the air. Even the drops in his own cell were gone.

"Hello?"

His voice scared him, so raspy he didn't recognize it. The table lamp was back, resting in the same place, revealing a black wall behind it. A plate and a tall glass sat just outside the bars, their shadows stretched far enough to touch the wall of his cell.

Cady steeled himself and sat up. His body felt weak-

er than ever. Even mornings after a major whiskey bend-
er didn't leave him this drained. Hunger had to be part
of it. He tried to stand, failed to find his balance, and
dropped to his hands and knees. *Fine,* he thought. He
crawled the short distance to the food and made his body
fold into a sitting position.

How long had he been in here? A week? Two?
Could the human body survive that long without food?

Cady's stomach growled. He reached through the
bars, intending to grab the plate, but completely of its
own free will, his hand seized the glass instead. The real
glass surprised him again. Hadn't Fritch considered how
easy it would be to shatter this frail thing and use the
shards to open his own veins?

Cady jolted toward the empty cell. Trilling *hadn't*
found a knife. He couldn't have. He'd used the glass, just
as Fritch intended. The cells had no doors. The only
way out of here was suicide. Fulfillment of Fritch's de-
mented idea about serving justice.

An ache grew in the back of his head. Instinctively,
Cady brought the glass to his lips. He smelled Fritch's
watermelon-sweetened tea. Stopped. His hand began to
shake. Withdrawal, already? What the hell was in this
stuff? He closed his eyes and remembered waking up in
rehab once. It wouldn't take much more to make him
feel that bad. He placed the glass on the floor and pushed
it away, being careful not to spill any.

Cady didn't know what Fritch made this shit with,
but it messed with his head more than anything he'd
ever heard of. Kept him busy by subjecting him to hor-

rific hallucinations, and too much of the stuff knocked him out like hospital-grade anesthesia. If he wanted to survive, he couldn't drink any more of it. Unfortunately, it wasn't like he could just switch to water for the duration of his stay. Staving off dehydration would mean carefully monitoring his intake. No more chugging.

He looked at the plate. Raw carrots and some kind of meat patty infused with spinach. His stomach rumbled again, but he wondered if Fritch put drugs in the food as well.

He used the bars to pull himself to standing. Every joint screamed in agony. Perhaps another side effect of the drug.

Still, his thoughts seemed pretty clear for the first time in a while. He gazed into Trilling's wide-open cell and pondered his situation.

He remembered the conversation over dinner that first night. Fritch insisted Cady's mystery plays needed to show justice being served. The old man had gotten heated talking about murderers going free on technicalities, and Ezzy had warned him off the subject. He'd been alluding to real life. Cady's accident had resulted in Priscilla's death, and her family told police they'd been fighting. They'd lied further and insisted Cady said he wanted to kill her. The police botched the Breathalyzer, though, and then failed to read him his rights. Later, encouraged by Priscilla's Dad passing money around, they'd held him and questioned him for a long time without his lawyer present.

Priscilla's family had been furious when the judge

threw out the case. While they were busy using the media to tear apart the police and the court system, Cady moved across the country. He told himself it was to avoid running into any of them, but in reality, he was trying to put distance between himself and the memories of the accident. While it was easy enough to dismiss a court case with a little paperwork, dismissing his guilt had taken quite a bit more. Alcohol. Lots of it. In the end, though, the image of Priscilla's torn-up body sitting beside him always returned in its full, high-definition glory.

He wondered how Fritch heard about it. Was the man related to Priscilla's family somehow? Maybe to one of the cops? The judge? Of all the court cases tossed out all across the country, what made Uncle Fritch focus on him?

And the better question was: Did Ezzy know? He doubted it. She'd seemed taken with him. Opening up to him about her desires, showing him her artwork, even pieces she deemed unfinished. She'd never held back in bed, either. No, Ezzy was innocent of Fritch's psychosis.

He only had to outsmart the old man, then.

Cady threw himself against the bars. Something shifted. He hadn't imagined that. He stepped back and took a good look at the setup. Cady tried to determine the nature of the building Fritch had brought him to. What kind of place would have two adjacent prison cells in a single room? Maybe a police station that had been left behind, or an abandoned zoo.

Cady placed his hand against the short wall on his left. It held a little bit of a chill. The other side of this wall was the area where Fritch appeared. The same area as the lamp. He moved to the back wall, sliding the cot aside as he went. These stones were colder, even a little damp. He looked carefully as he walked to the third wall and saw nothing that might be a walled-shut doorway for animals to enter and exit. Not a zoo, then. The far wall, where the other side of the bars were secured, was cold and damp as well.

This place *felt* like a cellar, which hinted at the possibility of an old police station, but why were there no doors on the cells? Fritch told him Ezzy was "back at the house." Could it have been a lie? Was it possible he was still in the decrepit old Tudor?

Cady re-crossed his cell to focus on the warmer wall. He pushed on it, but it yielded not at all. He poked at the mortar holding the stones in place. Solid. When he stepped toward the bars to inspect how they were attached, he noticed the mortar here was a lighter color.

He slid his hand between the bars and ran his fingers between the stones. Grittier than it should be.

Fritch must have leaned the bars against the end of the wall and then constructed a stone addition to hold them in place. What did Ezzy say he did for a living? Professor? Plumber? Pharmacist. That suggested Fritch would have very little experience with building a prison cell.

Cady seized one of the outermost stones holding the top horizontal bar in place. He pushed and wiggled. Thumped it with the palm of his hand.

Damned if a little mortar dust didn't sprinkle free.

Fritch mixed the mortar too dry.

Cady checked the other end of the cell. The man had drilled three holes into the stone and slid the horizontal bars in. It was possible he possessed the strength to accomplish all this by himself. He couldn't exactly hire help if he wanted to keep the prison's existence quiet. Maybe Ezzy *was* involved. Or maybe it was the servant who'd cooked their dinner. What was her name? Didn't matter.

If Fritch had mixed all the mortar the same way…

Cady returned to the workroom side of the cell and reached up through the bars again. He picked a stone that looked the least secured and wiggled it. He rubbed his finger along the mortar, and small crumbs came off. It was difficult to keep his balance on his tiptoes, but he kept working at the stone. Its movement seemed to be increasing microscopically. When his throat became too parched to continue, he lifted the glass and took a small sip of pink, swished it around to moisten everything, and then swallowed it slowly to dampen his throat.

His back threatened to erupt into crippling spasms when he lifted himself onto his toes again. A quick walk back and forth along the bars to help limber up, and he went back to it, wriggling the stone until it popped free.

He passed it from hand-to-hand around the three horizontal bars to place it on the floor, rather than risk the noise of dropping it. After another walk along the bars, he started on the next one.

Within a short time, seven stones were piled on the floor in front of his cell. Cady shoved against the top horizontal and felt a *skrik* as the bar shifted.

Encouraged, Cady started working on the stones holding the middle bar in place.

9

Hunger became urgent when Cady got to the low-est horizontal bar, the insistence of his dry mouth be-came paralyzing. Again. He sat cross-legged on the floor and chewed a carrot slowly, sucking hard to generate saliva. When it failed to alleviate his dry throat, he al-lowed himself one more sip of pink, sloshing it around as before. He'd sipped four or five times, but already a third of the liquid was gone.

He redoubled his efforts on the remaining stones. The first came away almost instantly. The second proved more stubborn. Frustrated, he grabbed a stone from the pile and hammered it at the one he was trying to free. The impact bruised his palm and fingers, but the stone fell out and dropped to the floor with a *clunk*. Cady gaped at it for a second. He should have done that earlier.

He swung his stone at the next, but it caught the tip of his middle finger. He yelped before he could stop himself. The panic subsided after a moment, and he looked at the injury. The nail was split down the middle. Blood pooled up and out.

He made a fist, and tendons trembled with exertion. His injured finger throbbed like a cartoon thumb. He reached up and shoved on the middle horizontal. It and the top one leaned outward and banged back, but the bottom didn't budge.

One more rock between him and freedom.

Pooling his energy, he seized the last stone and tried to force it out while shoving himself against the bars, hoping to pop it free like a rotten tooth.

Just like that, the stone came away in his hand.

He almost cheered but caught himself. He placed the stone on top of the pile, and, of course, it rolled off, clattering against other stones and the floor.

Above him, something thumped. The slam of a door? Someone running to check on him?

"No fair," Cady whispered.

He groaned as he rose to his feet, then paused to listen for a few moments. Upstairs remained quiet. Cady gripped the bars beneath the middle horizontal. His right hand didn't want to close all the way, but he fought through the pain and forced it. With a deep breath, Cady lifted and shoved at the bars with his chest.

They pushed out, but not enough for him to slide through. Almost, but not quite.

The other end of the bars were just stuck into holes

in the wall. Cady prepared himself again, but this time tugged the bars a little to the left.

Now, shoving forward again, he managed to slide the bars out another two inches.

Cady paused long enough to deny himself another sip of pink. He held his breath and then shoved himself at the opening between the wall and the bars. It was tight. While the middle bar scraped hard across his belly, the jagged edges of mortar scratched up his back pretty bad.

He was out.

He looked down at the floor lamp. Behind it stood a four-foot partition, solid black. Placed there, no doubt, to conceal the details of the room behind it. Cady tried to shove away the make-shift wall but discovered it was fastened to the floor. He lifted the floor lamp over it, barely registering a small masking taped "X" beneath it.

As he'd suspected, this area was a workplace. A single door stood ten feet away. Cady hoped it wasn't locked. Beside it on the wall was a light switch.

Cady took a step toward it. The lamp's cord reached full extension and popped out of whatever socket it had been plugged in to.

The darkness was complete.

Centipedes liked darkness.

He could hear them coming, minuscule feet clattering toward him, ready to climb his pants.

Cady swallowed his fear and slid his foot toward the door, keeping his left hand outstretched before him.

He slid another step. Another.

He barked in surprise when his hand thumped the wall. He slid his hand in circles across the plaster, extending his shoulder a little at a time, widening his arc until he found the doorjamb. Once there, he slid his hand the width of the door and started feeling the wall on the other side, again making tiny circles and widening as he went. He found the light switch when he accidentally flicked it on and off again. The flash drove into his eyes like nails.

He steeled himself, then turned on the light.

It took ages before he could crack open his eyes.

He turned to face the room. To the left stood the bars of Trilling's cell. Dozens of electrical pipes leaned in the corner against it. Cady suspected he could think about them for a week and not come up with a single reason for Fritch to have them.

From this angle, the slab of plywood behind the lamp was unpainted.

To the right stood the wall to his cell. In the corner, a card table held piles of light bulbs, plates, glasses, and one empty glass pitcher. Seeing it reminded him of his dry throat. For a moment, the urge to wriggle back through the bars to get ahold of his glass of pink seemed too strong to resist. It took two slow, steady breaths to move his thoughts past it.

His gaze wandered up over the card table. A patch of plaster ceiling showed a water stain, its edges yellow and dry, but darkening closer to the wall.

A long shape rose out of the stain, antennae wriggling. Cady blinked. Four more centipedes appeared on the ceiling and wall.

He turned back to the door and twisted the handle. Despite his fears, it wasn't locked. It opened right up.

Cady peered into the darkness. He didn't sense anything moving. He opened the door a little more, letting light from the prison room leak around him.

It revealed a narrow hallway. Across from him stood a plywood wall with decorative grooves running vertically every half a foot or so. It was painted a solid, god-awful aqua green. Needed Ezzy's touch.

To the left, the hallway stopped at another stone wall. Dead end. Cady walked to the right.

A little ways along, the hallway opened up to a larger area. The plaster ceiling ended and revealed exposed beams and insulation. Wires and pipes followed their busy paths here and there. This was definitely a cellar, but a cellar to what?

To the left, the plywood wall ended. Cady looked into the dark for a moment. He heard something scratching in there. His mind threw images of wriggling centipedes at him. He could almost feel them wrestling in his hair like when he was a kid. His breathing grew shallow as he gazed into the dark, too busy restraining his panic to look for a light switch.

He almost hollered when something unseen *whumped* a breathy bark at him. A furnace. The faint glow of fire shone near the floor but didn't illuminate anything. A utility room.

Cady turned around to face the remaining area of

the basement. Size-wise, this space seemed as large as the prison room he'd just left. Vague shadows of piles loomed deep inside. Cady took a step toward them, trying to see better.

He slapped at his face, scrubbed his palms over his eyes. *Cobwebs?* Something cold and metal thumped off his hand, which meant…

He caught the pull chain on his second try and tugged at it. Light flooded the room.

Fritch had been busy in here. He saw the jackhammer first, leaning in the far corner, then saw the hole. This room had been built with the same poured concrete as the rest of the cellar. Now it was torn up. Ragged chunks of stone and concrete piled high on the right side of the room. The exposed earth was churned and uneven, as if someone had been digging for treasure.

In the edge of his vision, Cady saw centipedes watching him throughout the pile of broken concrete. Antennae twitched in every dark hole. At the slightest sound, they'd come for him.

Cady took a step back. *Only the pink,* he told himself. He closed his eyes to calm down but now detected the faint scent of death. It was masked by something sweeter. As soon as he opened his eyes, he saw white powder mixed into the churned-up dirt. Four bags of lime were stacked just beyond the pile of broken cement.

Trilling was buried here.

How many others?

Things moved in the pile of concrete. Squirming bodies lengthened and skittered to the floor. Cady looked away, but the dirt started churning in the hole. Trilling, or more centipedes, crawling up from the grave.

Cady turned. The lights in the utility room had come on as well, and it took an instant to realize he had no escape here, either. To the left, though, running along the opposite side of the plywood wall, he saw the underside of a staircase.

He headed back toward the prison room, running his hand along the aqua wall. The first time his fingers drummed through a decorative groove, his split fingernail jolted and made him yelp.

Cady took another few steps while staring at his finger. His hand was streaked with blood, but all of it dried. The wound had stopped bleeding.

He froze when he saw the centipede watching him.

Not a whole one, he realized. Just a head. Poking out of the wall. No antennae, either.

He watched it for a few moments, waiting for it to finish materializing, but it didn't change. After maybe a full minute, Cady stepped closer.

It was a knob. Tiny and oblong, like a knob for a cabinet. He closely inspected the wall. Because of the poor light, he'd missed this section of plywood cut into a door. Its hinges were painted the same aqua green.

Cady pinched the knob and turned. A weak spring expanded inside. As the door opened, the dim light revealed a single step up onto a square landing. The staircase climbed to his right.

He felt the wall for a light switch. None. No hint of light peeked around a doorway up in the blackness, either.

No getting around this. Darkness or no, if he wanted his freedom, he had to climb the stairs.

He stepped up onto the landing. A small banister helped steady him, grounded him in reality. His mind tried to convince him that centipedes blanketed the walls to each side, but he refused to give in to panic. A quick twist of vertigo unbalanced him for a second. He attributed this to moving in the dark rather than to the pink. He couldn't afford to pass out now. Not so close to whatever this discovery would lead to.

He climbed. After a few stairs, he began to see a line of gray appear to the right, at eye-level. Light, distant and dim, peeking beneath a door. He climbed faster and reached the top of the stairs.

He wrapped his hand around the handle and pressed his ear to the door. Heard nothing. Wished he'd brought one of those electrical pipes as a weapon. Too late now, he decided to forge ahead unarmed.

10

Just as he steeled his nerve to twist the handle, something banged on the other side. He told himself it had nothing to do with him.

"BELLE!"

Fritch. Angry. Livid, even. Cady judged him to be standing over the prison room.

"BELLE, WHERE ARE YOU?"

Who the hell is Belle? Cady thought.

Cady's hand shook, rattling the doorknob. He released it before he could be heard. He listened for a response and heard how loud his breathing had gotten. He opened his mouth, trying to breathe quieter, and immediately his tongue and teeth dried out. Still, he forced himself to persevere. The centipedes that were—well, *not* surrounding him, since they didn't really exist—were listening, too.

And then Ezzy's voice came.

"I'm upstairs."

"Come down here, please."

Why had Ezzy answered? Was her name really Belle and not Esmeralda?

Cady decided he knew where he was. Fritch *had* lied to him. The prison had been built in the cellar of the Tudor.

It was impossible to tell for sure, but he thought the ceiling over the stairs kept the same incline, which meant another staircase above this one. The one he'd seen in the foyer that first night. If so, when he stepped out of the cellar, the front door would be to his right.

"Did you clean my study?"

Something small chattered just above Cady's head. He ducked, expecting a centipede to land in his hair, but nothing happened. He decided Ezzy had creaked a step while coming down.

"I think we both know the answer to that."

"God damn it."

"You promised me, Uncle."

"And god damn *you*." Cady was sure the old man was building himself into a rage. "I don't drink often, you know."

"You *promised* not to drink at all."

Fritch stammered for a bit. "You don't know what it's like!"

"Is that what you think?"

Cady remained blinded by darkness but turned his head up and to the right, where Ezzy must be standing, toward the bottom of the stairs. Her tone remained strong, fearless.

Cady feared enough for both of them. The memory of Fritch transforming into a man-sized centipede came flooding back. He tried to close his mouth, but his tongue seemed too large.

"Drink is what killed my mother."

"I—"

"Drink is what killed *your* wife."

"I know, but—"

"Drink is what's killing innocent people day in and day out, and murderers are going unpunished."

"Damnit, Belle. How can you expect me to cope?"

"You just *do* it. You just *do.*"

Cady pressed his hand to his chest. His heart had grown wings and was beating them against his ribs, trying to escape its own captivity. God, he needed a drink. Water. Pink. Anything. If he didn't get *something* into his system soon, he would pass out.

"I'm bringing Richard tomorrow," Ezzy—*Belle*— was saying. "I need you at the top of your game."

The front door. It would be to his right. He could make it, race outside, find a garden hose or something and drink his fill. Drink until his stomach sloshed.

"We can't—" Fritch said, and then Cady turned the handle and stepped out.

In the first instant, he recognized the ugly maroon and black wallpaper of the Tudor's foyer. In the next, he forced his eyes open wide because the light scratched his corneas, but he couldn't afford to close them. Fritch stood down the hall, his eyes wide, his mouth gaping.

Cady glanced at the stairs, caught the quickest glimpse of Ezzy with one hand over her mouth and the other resting on the wooden ball atop the newel post. His stepping out of the cellar like this must feel to her like seeing a ghost.

He bolted for the door, thinking only of finding water, and realized after he was moving that the kitchen behind him was far closer. Didn't matter. He had to get out of here.

Fritch stepped in front of him, hands upraised.

Cady barreled ahead, ducking at the last moment and shouldering into the big man's diaphragm, slamming him back against the door. Fritch slumped to his ass, wheezing.

Cady turned, looked into Ezzy's eyes.

"He's been lying to you." Cady barely recognized his own voice. His tongue was too big, his pronunciation too blunted. Still, she lowered her hand from her mouth and held it out to him.

"He's also been drugging you. Drugging us. Me. We…we need to go." He took a step toward her, then another. The whole house seemed to shift to the left. He recalled reading somewhere that dizziness was a sign of dehydration. It also heralded passing out. He shook his head.

Was Ezzy wearing a centipede scarf?

"You utter shit," Fritch growled. "How did you get out?"

Cady turned. Fritch had made his feet again. He pulled something from his pocket that looked very much like the garage door opener Ezzy had used the night they'd first arrived.

Cady wanted to attack, but the way Fritch's shirt pulsed around his body held him fast. Centipedes teemed under there. Some of them poked their heads out of his shirt cuffs, waved their antennae around.

The next instant everything exploded into a vast nova of white. Big as life, the word BUMP flashed in his mind, and when it cleared, he realized three things at once. One, something had struck the back of his head, hard. Two, he was falling. Three, the wooden ball from the top of the newel post was falling with him, and damned if it didn't look like the severed head of a giant centipede.

POONCHUCK

11

Cady snuggled in his pocket of darkness, safe from hundreds of kicking, flicking legs. The last thing he wanted to do was climb out, but the yelling was cracking open his skull. It was loud. Angry. It dug its claws into the sorest part of his head and tugged him toward consciousness, toward light, toward hopelessness.

The yelling continued.

Cady cracked his eyes open. Acknowledged the angled shadows on the wall, in all the same places he'd learned to expect. Vertigo threatened to make him vomit, so he closed them again.

He lay still, sightless, and tried to piece together what happened.

The foyer. Fritch.

Yelling again. Cursing. Vile, abhorrent sexual terms, repugnant slurs toward the mentally handicapped, and horrific offers of masochistic role-playing vibrated off the walls of the prison room.

The prison room. That's where he was.

Home, sweet home.

And he wasn't alone.

Someone was in Trilling's cell.

Someone who wouldn't stop yelling.

"LET ME OUT OF HERE!"

Cady cringed and tried to jerk away from the horrible hammering. He scrunched his eyes shut and clapped his hands over his ears. When the banging stopped, he cracked one eye and looked. The man was huge. He held the five-gallon bucket by its handle. It was cracked and dented beyond usefulness. With a grunt, the man smashed it against the bars once more, then hurled it into the corner of his cell.

He loosed another string of atrocities, culminating in a long bellow, which had to hurt his throat. Cady hoped Ezzy—*Belle*—wasn't near enough to hear this.

The man stopped yelling, content to clutch the bars and catch his breath.

Cady looked over.

"Awake, huh? Was beginning to think you's dead."

"How," Cady started, but couldn't make another sound around his swollen tongue. He tried again and grimaced. It felt like something in his throat folded. He sucked on his teeth, trying to work up enough saliva to speak. "How long I been out?"

The man snorted. "Damned if I know. Since I been here. LET ME THE FUCK OUT!"

"Don't think he can hear you," Cady rasped.

"That old fart? He can hear me just fine."

Cady tried to talk again, but his dry mouth wouldn't let him. He slid to the edge of his cot and let his legs drop to the floor, which pulled the rest of him down as well. He was careful to make his head land on his left forearm, but his ribs smacked against the concrete. When the worst of the pain passed, he struggled to his hands and knees.

Across the room, the new prisoner watched him.

A fresh glass of pink sat just outside the bars. With trembling fingers, Cady slid it through and leaned back on his legs while he drank.

Sip, he told himself. He had to physically pull the glass away from his mouth to stop. Some of it splashed on his shirt, and he swallowed before he could swish it around. He cursed himself, then took a small bit more and swished it around properly.

It moistened his mouth just enough.

Cady returned the new man's gaze. "Name's Cady," he said.

"So what?"

Cady stared at him. The man was tall. Six feet plus, easy. He wore ratty jeans and a navy blue button-down work shirt. No nametag over the shirt pocket. The man's hairy feet were bare against the concrete. Cady scanned the cell but didn't see his shoes anywhere. Fritch must have taken them.

The guy had a five o'clock shadow that was the same dark black as the oily hair hanging off his head. A small scar nicked the corner of his eye, giving his face a cruel tone. Cady was about to ask outright for the man's name but realized it didn't matter. It wasn't like Fritch was erecting headstones for his victims.

The image of the burial room came back to him, complete with boiling dirt as the centipedes wriggled up. He would do anything to not end up under this house. Even risk life in prison, a real prison, by murdering Fritch at the very next opportunity.

"How long have you been here?" Cady asked.

"You stupid or something? I told ya, I don't know."

Cady tried to stand. The ache in his head became a physical thing that tried to push him back down. He gritted his teeth and powered through the movement anyway, then leaned on the middle horizontal and rested his head against the bars.

The other man watched him.

"You gonna die, or what?"

"Feels like it," he said. "I think that's what Fritch wants, anyway."

"What the fuck is a Fritch?"

"Big guy? Short, curly hair?"

The other man scoffed again. "You mean Gary? Big pansy?"

"Gary?"

"Engersoll. Former Professor. Had a breakdown after his wife died. Got caught assaulting drunk students at a frat party."

"Told me his name was Fritch."

"What'd he tell you his daughter's name was?"

"You mean his niece?"

"Niece," the man said with a grin. "Five-seven? Longish black hair? Good body, even though her ass is getting fat?"

Cady swallowed. He was describing Ezzy, though Cady would never accuse her of having a fat ass. "That's Belle, his niece."

"Belle? How fucked up is that? Her name is Susan. She's the one who brought me here. She called me in for a job."

"Job?"

The man looked at him. "Off someone."

Cady swallowed. "She wanted to...*off* me?"

"No idea. She gave me tea with this funky sweetener in it. Next thing I knew, I was on the floor with rats crawling all over me." He shuddered.

"Rats?"

The man glared at him. "I don't like rats, okay? Dirty little fuckers." He shuddered again and waved his hand in the air. "Forget it. Dame is worse than he is. Crazy bitch."

Cady nodded. He'd seen Ezzy when he escaped. She'd answered to Belle, so he figured that was her real name. He'd tried to take her with him. She'd been behind him when—

"Name's Poonchuck," the man said.

"So what?" Cady stepped back and sat on his cot.

The man started hollering again, just as loudly as before.

Poonchuck was a weird name. Native American,

maybe? If the guy were any nicer, Cady might ask, but it already seemed this guy was crazier than Trilling. Only way more violent.

Violent. "I bet you're strong," Cady said when he quieted, maybe ten minutes later.

Poonchuck flipped him off.

Cady sat up on the edge of the cot. He pushed a wave of dizziness away, glanced at his half glass of pink, then refocused. "I broke out of here. Yesterday."

"Right."

"Fritch ain't exactly a blue-collar kind of guy. And it ain't like he went and got permits to build a prison in his cellar, so he's got to do all this work himself to keep it secret. He mixed the mortar too dry. I busted up the masonry holding the bars in place."

"Really." Poonchuck's tone was pure skeptic, but he looked along the bars to the wall just the same.

"It looks like…" Cady stood too quickly, groaned, and collapsed back onto the bed. He took a few breaths and tried again. This time he kept his balance, though he felt a little wobbly. He thought through every move it took to cross to the bars and lean against them.

"It looks like he repaired it."

Poonchuck wandered to the opposite side of his cell and picked up the bucket.

"You didn't do shit," Poonchuck said.

Cady looked at him. "What are you talking about? Of course, I did."

"Look at you. You're wasting away. You couldn't've broken up a stone wall with your bare hands. Don't matter how dry the mortar was."

"I did, though." Cady held up his right hand, noticed the bandage for the first time. It was dull looking, like it had been applied a while ago. His stomach gave a grumble.

Poonchuck shook his head some more. "I don't know you from old man shit," he said. Before Cady could ask what that meant, he continued. "For all I know, you're working for her, trying to drive me crazy."

"What?"

"I'm on to you," the man said, pointing at him. "Engersoll said he wants me to commit suicide. Ain't gonna happen. He can't make me, and you can't, either. And I ain't confessing shit, so you can get that fat notion right out of your head."

"Confess to what?"

"Fuck you."

Cady wanted to ask what the man had done, but asking wouldn't lead to freedom.

Poonchuck blew an exasperated breath and dropped the busted bucket with a clatter.

"What are we supposed to do when we have to take a piss?"

Cady just looked at him.

"Is that..." Poonchuck looked at the bucket, swore again, and kicked it against the wall.

Poonchuck crossed the cell to stand in front of him. He turned to look where the bars were fastened. He reached through and seized a stone. He barked in pain and jerked his hand back.

"You fuck! You *are* working for him!"

"What happened?"

"As if you didn't know. Fuck you."

Poonchuck stuck his hand through the bars and flicked his wrist across the expanse between the cells. Droplets of blood speckled the floor, almost reaching all the way to Cady's cell.

The man had cut himself, which didn't make any sense. Cady reached through the bars and laid his palm on a stone. He yelped and pulled his hand back. Blood welled up from half a dozen small cuts. Something glinted on the stones. Cady reached out again, used just the tip of his finger to poke where the light shone. The pain was immediate.

Broken glass. Fritch either mixed it in with the mortar or coated the stones with some kind of epoxy and then pressed broken glass onto it. There was no way either of them could withstand enough lacerations to free these bars. Their hands would be chewed to stubs long before they finished.

Fritch probably considered this a bonus. Now there was another way for his prisoners to slit their wrists.

"Dammit." He slumped against the bars. He wouldn't be getting out of here again.

He watched the tall man pace in his cell. When he couldn't bear the dryness in his mouth, he bent down, took a sip, and swished it around.

Poonchuck saw him, then reached between his own bars and pulled his own glass of pink in.

"Don't want to drink too much of that."

Poonchuck kept eye contact with him while he took one, two, three big swallows. "Fuck you," he said again. His voice rasped.

"Do you see a door anywhere on these bars, man? I'm a prisoner, just like you. Just like the guy before you. And that shit," he pointed to the glass in the man's hand, "is drugged."

Poonchuck stared at him. Cady stared back. He ignored the small twitches the man's shirt made. He even ignored the way the man's hair seemed to be moving on its own.

"What do you mean 'the guy here before me'?"

"Trilling. Crazy sonuvabitch."

Poonchuck paused a moment more. "What happened to him?"

"Just what Fritch wanted. Suicide. He's buried under the floor on the other side of your cell."

The man scoffed. "You're shitting."

Cady stared back. The shadows of the bars were starting to writhe again. The sight sent a wash of tingling across his back and made his breathing quicken. If he downed the rest of the pink, it would knock him out. Tempting.

"What do you mean, 'buried'?"

"'Scuse me?"

"How do you know what that old shit did when you were asleep?" Distrust radiated from him, but some other thought seemed to be working itself into his brain.

Cady sighed. "I told you. I got out. I loosened the stones until they came free, and I left. I found the room next door, where he's burying people."

"He's burying people inside the house?"

"*Beneath* the house. He jackhammered the floor over there, and he's buried people. He's got plenty of room for more, from the looks of it."

Poonchuck shook his head. "Nah. Nice try, though. Lackey."

"Don't be stupid. Why would I tell you how to escape if I was working for him?"

"You calling me stupid?"

Cady paused. "Well, you sure as hell aren't being smart."

Poonchuck struck the bars three times fast, cursing at him the whole time. When he stopped, he tried to ignore his hands while he flexed them. Bruised, no doubt.

"You're still not being smart," Cady taunted.

Poonchuck bellied up to the bars, stuck his arm through, and pointed at him. "You better hope I never get out of here, motherfucker. I will rip your fucking head off and feed it to you!"

Cady didn't blink. "How are you going to feed me my head when my mouth is on it?"

"What?"

"Tell you what. I'll stop calling you stupid when you start thinking and talking sense."

"I'll kill you, you fuck."

"Have to get out of there first."

Poonchuck roared, stepped to the side, and kicked the stone wall right beside the middle horizontal. Cady swore the impact knocked a wave of centipedes off the other side. He told himself they weren't scrambling towards him. Meanwhile, Poonchuck fell onto his cot in a ball, moaning and holding his foot.

"Forget you weren't wearing shoes?"

"You're a dead man. But first, I'm going to make you watch while I kill your friend. And the fat-assed bitch."

"You still have to get out of there. And then you'll have to get *me* out of *here*." If looks could kill, Cady would be ready for a dirt spot beside Trilling. "You think it over. I'll be on my cot, collecting my thoughts."

Cady stretched out. He'd drunk too much pink too quickly. The centipedes were massing on the ceiling. He couldn't actually see them crawling up the walls, so he figured they were following the shadows of the bars. His hands throbbed. His right middle finger, where he'd smashed it with the stone, and his left palm, where it had been punctured by the glass.

He closed his eyes and focused on the pain to distract himself while the hallucinations gathered in strength.

Poonchuck didn't breathe so much as he seethed. He sensed the mean bastard staring at him and twice opened his eyes to make sure he was still secure in his cell. He was, of course. Cady ignored the scritching and scratching around him and waited.

12

The squeak of cot springs alerted Cady that Poonchuck was up to something. Cady listened to the steady noise but couldn't imagine what the man was doing.

He opened one eye. Poonchuck stood at the end of his cot, wiggling it back and forth. He'd thrown the mattress to the other end of the cell.

Cady sat up with a groan, but Poonchuck ignored him. He bent over and fiddled with something on the underside of the cot. The metal side support disconnected from the footboard. It drooped while Poonchuck worked at the nut and bolts on the other end. A few moments later, that side support dropped free as well.

"Never thought of that," Cady said.

Poonchuck grinned. "Now who's stupid?"

Cady nodded the point while Poonchuck lifted the

83

footboard, a solid metal pipe bent in the shape of a "U." It reminded Cady of a giant cartoon magnet.

Poonchuck held it sideways and stuck the feet outside the bars, close to where they were encased. He shoved against the stone. The crackling glass made Cady shudder.

The stones didn't give.

"You can do it," Cady said.

"Fuck off."

"Just get me out of here. Together, we can take him."

"I ain't doing shit for you. Shut it."

Poonchuck pushed the lower leg against the wall and pulled the top leg away, using it as a lever to hammer against the stones. On his first swing, flecks of mortar flew away, as did shards of glass.

Cady bent over his cot and pulled up the mattress. The footboard was connected by two bolts on each side. He reached under and tried to unscrew one, but with his sore hands, he couldn't budge it. Explained why Poonchuck had wiggled the bed back and forth for so long. He'd loosened them up first.

When Fritch saw what Poonchuck had done, he'd pour epoxy on the bolts, making them impossible to undo with bare hands.

Cady reached under the cot again. One of the springs sprouted antennae and darted for his hand. Cady screamed and fell backward, landing on his ass and bumping the five-gallon bucket hard enough to send a slosh of piss over the side, splashing his arm.

"WHAT?" Poonchuck yelled. "A RAT?"

Cady kept his eyes shut, forced himself not to throw up. He shook his head, telling himself he hadn't seen anything. The pink was messing with him again.

"Don't play with me," Poonchuck said. "If you saw one, tell me."

"I didn't see a rat."

"Goddammit, don't lie to me."

"The pink heightens our fears, man. It makes us hallucinate. Drink enough of it, you'll be seeing rats everywhere."

"You telling me you don't hear them?"

Cady could hear a light buzzing, which he'd grown accustomed to. *The pink.*

"Can't hear a thing," Cady lied.

Poonchuck's gaze went to the ceiling. "Must be a million of them." He went back to pounding the stones with the footboard, his voice tinged with panic.

"HEY, ASSHOLE! LET ME OUT!"

Cady stood, using the bars for leverage.

The first stone fell free from Poonchuck's cell.

Cady sat on the edge of his bed and watched the man work. He breathed through his mouth, as his tongue was too big to close his teeth around. Damned if he would swallow any more pink, though. The bars to his cell already looked segmented, and if he took his eyes off them, he was sure they'd wriggle around.

"Done," Poonchuck said.

The stones from the top and middle horizontal had been knocked away. Cady must have zoned out big-time. Whether because of a side effect of the pink or of dehydration, he didn't know.

Poonchuck leaned the footboard against the wall, then shoved himself against the bars. With a loud *crack*, they moved.

Cady watched a smile spread across Poonchuck's face. He took a few steps back to get some momentum and then winked at him.

A doorknob rattled, a hinge squeaked, the overhead lights flicked on. Fritch hollered, "Good news, everybody!" at the same instant Poonchuck took off.

He hit the bars with all his weight. This time the crack was louder. The bottom horizontal popped out of the wall in an explosion of stones and jagged pieces of mortar.

Fritch cursed as Poonchuck drove his left arm between the bars and the wall and began shoving his body through the space. A deep, animalistic growl rumbled from the tall man as he fought through. The bars didn't want to let him pass, but Poonchuck shoved and roared, making himself fit.

"Freeze, asshole!" Fritch yelled.

Poonchuck popped free of his cell and turned toward the voice. The glass shards on the wall had torn up Poonchuck's shirt and pants, as well as the skin beneath. Cady counted at least eleven expanding spots of blood.

"You," Poonchuck grumbled.

"Don't move."

Poonchuck paused a moment. "The fuck you got

in your shirt?"

The overhead lights flicked off, leaving the low table lamp and its crooked shadows again. Cady had a second to marvel that the flying stones hadn't shattered the bulb.

"I will shoot you, Mister Poonchuck."

"I'll kill you first."

Poonchuck dove to his right, out of Cady's sight, and the crash of electrical pipes almost drowned out the sound of Fritch's first shot.

Cady slapped his hands over his ears.

Silver centipedes, long and straight, scurried toward his cell. One of them bumped the lamp, stirring the shadows, giving him another glimpse of the masking tape "X."

Another gunshot.

Cady watched the bugs in front of his cell, waiting for them to move. He blinked, but they'd become electrical pipes again. Half a dozen of them. Close to the bars.

He dropped to one knee, seized two, and yanked them inside.

"Don't!" Fritch yelled, and for a second Cady thought the old man was talking to him, but the shadows moved, and he realized Poonchuck had made his feet again. "Stop!"

Another gunshot. Another.

Cady lifted his mattress and laid the pipes on the springs. They were just short enough to fit catty-corner.

A wave of centipedes crashed against the bars. Cady whirled to see Poonchuck stumbling along the hallway between the cells. One more shot rang out, dull, the sound of a cork popping off a champagne bottle, and

Poonchuck's nose exploded into a red blossom as he tumbled backward, slammed his head on the stone wall.

Cady gaped at him. Counted one, two, three bloody holes in his chest. One of Fritch's shots must have missed. The bloodstains on Poonchuck's shirt didn't grow. Cady knew from TV shows this meant his heart had stopped.

Fritch stepped into view, his body rigid, his handgun still pointed at Poonchuck's unmoving form. He stepped around the partition and the lamp to stand just inside the hallway. His shadow filled the room. Cady watched him inspect the carnage Poonchuck had made of his cell.

"Damn it all to hell." Fritch took a huge breath and ran a trembling hand through his curly hair. He held his eyes open wide, as if staving off tears. "What a mess."

"*You* made it," Cady said.

Fritch whirled on him, gun barrel wide open and staring like a glassy, black eye. A centipede frolicked on Fritch's forearm, scurrying around his wrist and the gun, tracing senseless patterns. Fritch acted like it wasn't happening.

"The pole," he said.

Cady blinked. "Welsh, actually."

Fritch looked confused.

"My name. Most people think it sounds Irish, but it's short for 'Cadell,' which is Welsh."

"The hell are you…do you not see the gun, dear boy? Didn't you just watch me…" He glanced sideways at Poonchuck's body. "…shoot that man?"

"You mean Poonchuck?"

The centipede paused atop Fritch's wrist and raised its head to regard him. Its antennae flailed around if *tasting* the air.

"You know who he was?"

Cady ignored Fritch's pulsing shirt. He ignored the way his pencil-thin beard seemed to drum insectile legs against his cheek. "He told me his name."

"And it didn't mean anything to you?"

Cady shrugged. "Should it?"

"You animals should be more attentive to your own kind. This…beast…killed an innocent woman several years ago. Ripped her arms off. Both of them. Watched her bleed to death while he was high on PCP."

"Let me guess. He didn't do *time* for the *crime*."

Fritch's lips pursed. "Fucking lawyers."

"So you mete out your own judgment?"

"Why shouldn't I? I can. I can get away with it, too. And to top it off, I'm ridding the world of cutthroats and criminals."

"Except you want to kill me because of an accident."

"You were drunk. What you did to Priscilla was no accident."

Cady stared at him. Fritch's beard had become a single long centipede, chasing its tail in circles around his face.

"And I have no intention of killing you. You're go-ing to do that all by yourself."

"Just like Poonchuck, huh?"

"He gave me no choice." Fritch swallowed and

glanced at the dead man. Even in the weak light, Cady could see how pale he was.

"You've never killed anyone before, have you?"

"I can't allow you to keep the pole," Fritch said.

"What pole?" He glanced down and saw the centipedes leaking out from the man's pants cuffs. He tried to will the images away, but the pink was too strong.

"Just hand over the pole, you animal."

"You want me to just give it to you?"

"If you would."

"I won't."

"*I've* got the gun!"

"But it won't be suicide if you shoot me."

"I wanted Poonchuck to kill himself. You saw what I did to him."

Cady looked at the dead man. Something stringy was burrowing out of the hole where Poonchuck's nose used to be. His left eye gazed ahead, the eyelid propped open by a twisted nugget of gore. Cady wanted to believe he was still breathing, but the bloodstains on his shirt remained unchanged.

"I think I'll just keep the pipe, sorry, the *pole*, thanks all the same."

Fritch blinked. "I can shoot you where it will hurt. Through the kneecap. The elbow."

Cady held his hands out and spread his legs. "And I'll still have the pipe."

Fritch remained silent for a few beats, and then his face broke into a smile. "I almost forgot the reason I came down here. It's time for your tea. Perhaps you would—"

"Trade for the pipe? Keep your tea." Cady used every ounce of willpower he had to keep from salivating at the mention of tea. Along with the desire came the first probing fingers of a headache. He looked at the glass inside his cell and found it on its side, liquid puddled on the floor. When had that happened?

Fritch dropped his gun hand. "Too bad you didn't search this room a little harder yesterday. I keep this," he held up the gun, "hidden in here for emergencies. If you'd found it, you could have just shot us and been on your way."

Cady swallowed. "Well, now I know it's here for next time."

Fritch laughed. "There won't be a next time." He turned on his heel and walked out of Cady's line of sight. "You had one chance at escape, and you blew it." Cady heard liquid being poured and his thirst exploded.

Fritch came back to stand in front of the bars, closer this time, but not so close he couldn't dart away if Cady tried anything.

"You want this, don't you?"

Cady licked his lips. He couldn't help it.

"Sure you do. It's the watermelon sweetener. Great stuff. Addicting, don't you know?"

Cady squinted and forced his arm to stay by his side.

"Of course, if you're not interested..." Cady couldn't believe it when Fritch brought the glass to his own lips and slurped.

"I've been without longer than you," he said. "But

I just take tiny sips, here and there, every hour or so. Just enough to maintain my good humor. You have no idea how stressful it is, keeping murderers and cutthroats locked up in your basement."

"I'll just bet," Cady said.

"I will give you the rest of this," Fritch said. "Just as soon as you place the pole on the floor and kick it through the bars."

Cady swallowed. He tried to look Fritch in the eye but couldn't pry his gaze from the glass. The color was magical, brilliant. A shade of pink to rival the most romantic sunsets. His voice rasped. "What pole?"

Fritch responded by bringing the glass to his lips and gulping the rest. Cady's lungs deflated, bringing his shoulders and head down with them.

"Hits the spot," Fritch smacked his lips.

Cady reached out, unable to stop himself. He didn't want Fritch to know his torments were having an effect, so he forced his hand to close around the bars. He hoped his expression looked aloof, but if Fritch handed him the empty glass, Cady would lick the inside as far as his tongue would stretch.

"I never knew this stuff caused hallucinations," Fritch said. "Imagine my surprise when I discovered my late wife watching me from outside the study window."

"You're afraid of your wife?"

"Well, she's been dead a long time. I went outside to look for her in the bushes. When I got there, she'd gone inside to stare down at me through the same window."

All of the man's hair had turned into centipedes. They swirled and scurried all over his head, an occasional one darting across his face.

Fritch kicked the rest of the fallen electrical pipes back toward the corner behind Poonchuck's cell. Then he walked off. Cady leaned against the bars, trying to see through the gloom where the man had gone. A voice in his head suggested it was a good thing he'd gone, but a louder voice insisted it was very bad indeed. A few seconds later, he heard the man pouring another glass of pink. Cady's knees almost buckled.

"You look like you could use this," Fritch said. His hair was back. It looked like all the centipedes had crawled under his shirt, where they frolicked and played.

Cady reached for the glass. He didn't want to, but his hand moved of its own accord.

"Absolutely, dear boy. But first, we need to resolve the matter of that pole."

Cady nodded.

"That's all that's standing between you and this wonderfully refreshing drink."

Cady nodded some more. Turned to glare at his cot. *Under there,* he thought. Those electrical pipes were keeping him from relief.

"You just return the pole to me, and you can be quaffing this down while I pour you another. You'd like that, wouldn't you?"

Cady nodded while he stepped toward the cot. He tried to remember what he'd wanted them for, anyway.

Them.

Fritch hadn't asked for *both* of them. He didn't realize Cady had *two*. Cady played the incident back in his head. There had been a mess of pipes on the ground, but Fritch was too busy taking out Poonchuck to pay close attention to what Cady was doing. He'd pulled two pipes through the bars simultaneously. Fritch assumed it had only been one.

Cady reached under the mattress, felt both pipes resting together, and shoved his fingers between them. He brought one out, held it up for Fritch to see.

"Good. Good man. Now I want you to lower it and hold it in both fists."

Cady did as he was told.

"Slowly. Slowly. Place it on the floor in front of you." Cady kept his eyes on the glass in Fritch's hand as he laid the pipe on the bare concrete. "Excellent. Stand up, and with your feet, turn the pipe so it's pointed toward your cell bars."

Cady did this, too.

"Push the pipe between the bars and away from you."

Cady started but needed to clutch the bars to keep his balance. Once the pipe was through, Cady gave it an extra swift kick, sending it across the corridor. He'd hoped to send it all the way through the bars of Poonchuck's cell, but as luck would have it, the thing arrowed off one of the bars with a *clang*.

"Good shot," Fritch said.

He crouched over and lifted the pipe, then tossed it behind him, where it clattered with the others.

"Okay, okay, don't nag," Fritch said, holding the pink out to him.

"I'm not nagging," Cady told him.

Fritch pulled the glass back again. "You understand why I couldn't let you keep it?"

Cady nodded. He tried not to think about the second pipe secreted beneath the mattress, afraid Fritch would be able to read the information on his face.

Cady reached for the glass. Fritch opened his hand. The glass fell in super-slow-motion, shattering outward like a blast of fireworks.

"You are such a klutz, Cady."

Cady couldn't argue. He couldn't look away from the puddle.

"You got pink all over my shoes."

"Please," Cady said.

Fritch raised his eyebrows. "Please go clean up before I pour you more? That's so kind of you."

"No, no." Cady shook his head.

"I'll be back in a bit, and then we'll get you taken care of. I don't want this stuff to stain my shoes."

Cady dropped his head. Near the floor, the bottoms of the bars were starting to segment below the lowest horizontal. They gyrated back and forth, mocking him.

"When Belle gets home, I'll bring you more pink."

"Who's Belle?"

Fritch froze. Turned to him with a smile. "I'm sorry?"

"Who is Belle?" Cady met his gaze. He pointedly ignored the antennae reaching up from the man's shirt to caress his chin. "Who is she?"

"Don't know what you're talking about, dear boy."

"Poonchuck mentioned you had a daughter."

"Poonchuck was crazy." Fritch circled his finger around his ear. "Loco in the brain. And a murderer, as well. He'd say anything to get what he wanted."

Cady nodded. The segmentation of the bars spread upwards. The bars below the middle horizontal began to wiggle. "Where's Ezzy, then?"

Fritch sighed. "You might as well know, son. There is no 'Ezzy.' The woman you knew as 'Ezzy' is my daughter Belle, short for Annabelle. Her mother, my wife, was killed by an animal like you. Belle is the one who thought all this up."

Cady stared at him. He tried to make sense of the words, ran his hand through his hair, and winced when he touched the bruise on the back of his head.

"My daughter did a number on you, didn't she?"

Cady couldn't respond. He didn't feel blood in his hair, which meant there wasn't a hole in his skin the centipedes could squirm into. Or out of.

Fritch looked at Poonchuck's body for a long time, then sighed. "Never let it be said I am completely heartless," Fritch said. "I'll leave you with something after all."

He disappeared behind the wall, and Cady heard him pouring again. First one glass, then another.

Cady tried to clear his thoughts. Fritch stood before the bars holding a glass of pink in each hand.

"I am not going to drink with you," Cady said.

"Nor would I ask you to, foolish boy. *Both* of these are for you." He bent down and placed both glasses within reach of the bars. "I shall retire to my study to await Belle's return. And I won't be drinking any more of this tonight. At all. Belle will be unhappy Poonchuck... died while she was away. She will be less happy to learn I killed him myself, but I need her help to clean this mess up and prepare the cell again. I'll need you asleep, so drink up."

Cady nodded.

"Or you could take your own life. I'm sure Priscilla will be waiting for you on the other side."

Cady glanced at the shattered glass stuck to the stones. Slicing himself open would be so easy. For once, the thought of suicide didn't seem like a bad prospect.

Fritch nodded once, then walked off.

Cady listened to be sure the door closed. He wondered if Fritch had remembered to re-hide the gun, or if he'd left it on the serving table behind his cell. Then he figured it didn't matter. Wherever it was, it wouldn't do him any good. He wouldn't be getting out of this cell.

He bent down, reached through the bars, and pulled one of the glasses inside.

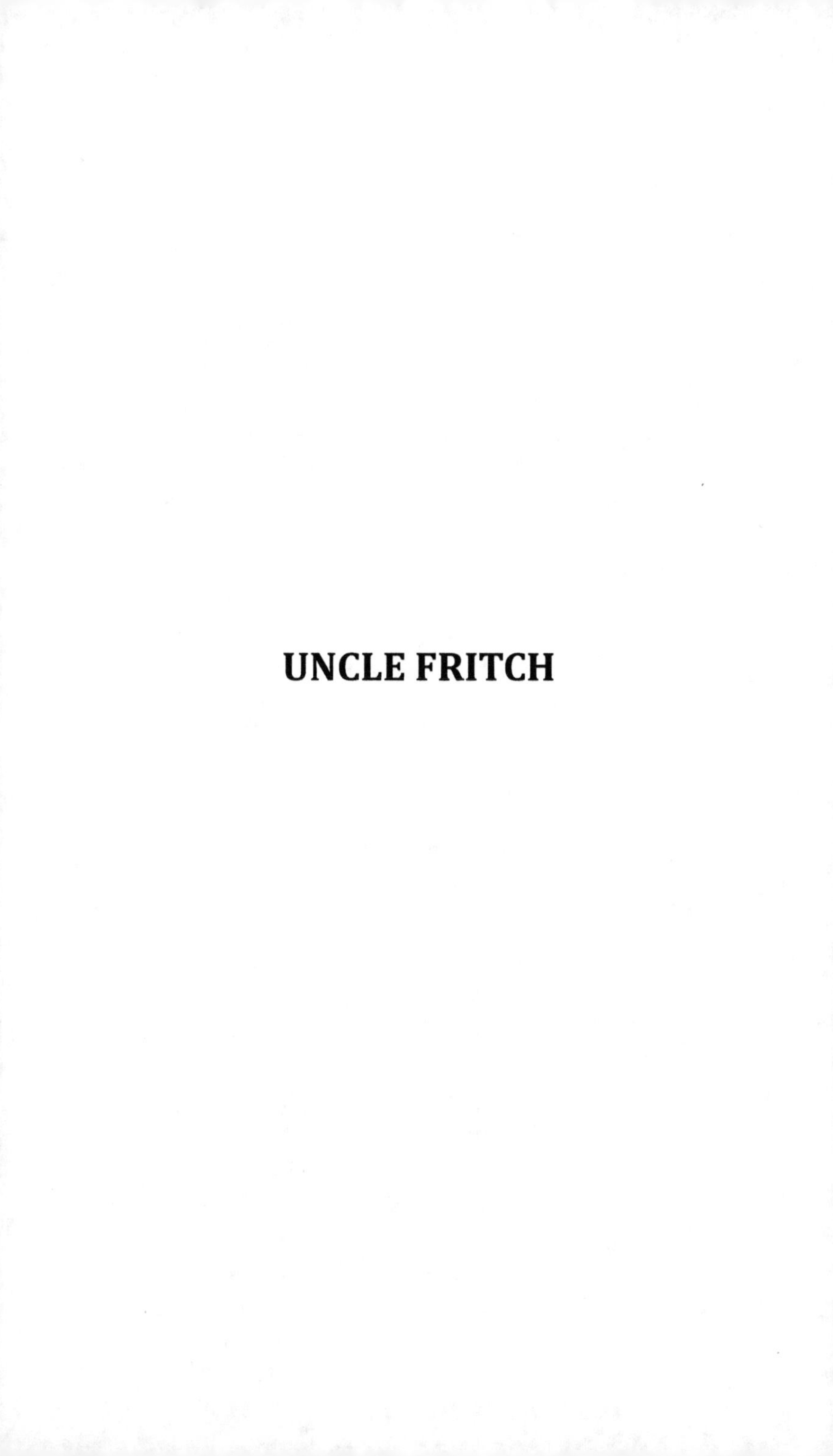

UNCLE FRITCH

13

Cady sat on his bed and let a tiny sip of pink slosh around his mouth, guiding it under his tongue and over his teeth. He even dipped his finger in and snorted the moisture into his sinus cavities because they were so tight he was sure they'd tear open. When he felt a little better, he held the glass up in front of him. Three-quarters full. He placed it on the floor, near the bars, where the full glass waited for him.

Maybe chugging both at the same time would be fatal. He doubted it, though. Fritch and Ezzy, or Belle, or whoever she was, seemed intent on blood and pain and regret and anguish. Death by a simple overdose would be too kind. Trilling, he supposed, had made them very happy.

Cady sighed. He thought he gained an incredible advantage by concealing the second pipe, but what good had it done him? He could do nothing with it. He'd be no worse off if he cut his losses and tossed it through the bars at the pile on the floor.

Cady dug it out from under the mattress. It was solid enough to beat a man with, light enough and narrow enough to wield through the bars. Even if he beat Fritch to death with it, he'd still be trapped.

He lay back on the bed and held the pipe to his chest. Told himself it was *not* wriggling against him. *Just the effect of the tea.* Certainly, the pipe wasn't growing legs.

Something moved.

Poonchuck.

The crazy bastard had been biding his time until Fritch left. Now that the coast was clear, he was going to rise up and help free Cady.

He raised his head.

Poonchuck's body remained on the floor. All four bullet holes accounted for. One eye still half-open. The bars of his cell, though, swayed like seaweed in a lackadaisical tide. Segmented from floor to ceiling now, each one had sprouted tiny bristles, which would evolve into legs before long.

Cady dropped his head back on the mattress. Blinked. He could hear rain. The realization caused his throat to constrict hard. He sat up and reached for the pink before he decided to.

He saw his hand, stopped it in mid-air before it reached the glass. Smears of blood from his torn palm had worked their way around to the back. His thirst fell away.

Something wasn't right.

He straightened his back. Rested his left hand palm-up on his lap, clutched the standing electrical pipe in his right hand like a scepter. Like he was a king.

King of the centipedes.

Something scratched in the workroom. He tried not to think about the other pipes transmuting into squiggling insects. In a few minutes, he would be ankle deep in the things, fighting them away with his bare hands because the pipe he held would turn as well. He counted himself lucky it hadn't wrapped itself around his wrist already.

He looked at it. No segments yet, thank God.

Ezzy could paint segments on it. Believable ones.

More tea. That's what he needed. Dehydration was mucking up his thoughts. A little bit more would help him sort things out. He picked up the glass and raised it until he could smell the sweetener. One deep breath later, and apathy folded through him like an old friend.

He drank. Chugged two swallows, three.

Stopped.

Third of a glass left.

Ezzy could paint.

He put the glass down and looked at the ceiling. It put a crick in his neck, so he laid back the way he had been, again clutching the pipe to his chest.

The stones on this end of the ceiling were darker than the other side. *Shadows?* Maybe.

Cady stared at them. The air buzzed around him. He ignored it. He focused on the sound of rain.

It seemed musty in here. Damp.

Cady raised his right hand and laid it against the stone wall of the cell.

The bandage around his middle finger came away wet.

Rainwater seeped through.

He remembered the key Ezzy painted in her cup holder. Even after he'd known it wasn't real, he tried to pick it up. She'd duped him good. Worked a miracle with her little paintbrush.

When he was out of his cell, he'd seen the work-room ceiling. It was made of sheetrock. Water damaged.

Cady stood the pipe up on his belly. It was almost long enough to reach the ceiling. He jammed it upward. Instead of the hard *click* of metal striking rock, he heard a *thump*, like a fingernail poking Styrofoam.

"No way," Cady whispered. He felt his first smile since he woke up in this dungeon.

He pulled the pipe back and drove it upward again, slamming it against the ceiling as hard as he could. Bits rained down on him. He scrunched his eyes, wiped his face with his hand while the pipe dropped to the floor. When he looked again, a jagged white hole peeped from the center of what appeared to be a solid stone in the ceiling.

This work far surpassed what Ezzy had done on the key. The stone ceiling was so good, so perfectly rendered, he'd never even thought to question the veracity of what he was seeing. It also explained why Fritch kept one dim light on the spot marked with an "X." Keeping just the right perspective would reduce the chance a prisoner would notice the stones threw no shadows of their own.

Cady stood. The ceiling was almost two feet beyond his reach.

He placed the pipe on the floor and rolled it against the bars. Folded the mattress over and moved it to the other end of his cell. Turned the cot onto its side.

He leaned his weight on the side rail and lifted himself. There was some give to it, but he thought if he stayed closer to the headboard it would hold him long enough for what he needed.

He got a knee on top and pulled himself up. Metal crunched bone, his left hand and right middle finger protested every ounce of support he made them carry. Around him, the shadows of the bars wriggled tiny feet. He rose up on the bed frame and brushed sheetrock with his fingers, not stone. He could feel the texture of the paint, the sponginess of the ceiling. The water damage was extreme.

He tried to remember what Fritch said he'd be doing tonight. He'd said pointedly he wasn't going to drink any more. *At all.* Cady hadn't asked. The man had offered the information without any prodding. As if he was trying to convince himself. Cady had firsthand knowledge of such self-delusional tactics. He'd learned about them in AA during the three weeks he'd tried to attend.

Ezzy had thrown away Fritch's Scotch. They'd been fighting about it when he'd made his trip upstairs. With no alcohol in the house, it wasn't surprising Fritch would start drinking the pink himself. Any port in a storm, as it were. But had he drunk enough of it to pass out? If so, he'd be oblivious to Cady hammering his way to freedom with the pipe. After all, Cady remembered nothing about Fritch sealing him in with mortar and stones. *Either* time.

Something moved behind him. He dropped off the cot frame and turned to Poonchuck. Three inches of centipede had wiggled out of the hole in his face.

"Not now," Cady said.

He turned his eyes to the ceiling and started to plan.

14

Soon, he was making good headway. The water-damaged sheetrock crumbled off with barely any effort on Cady's part. It was wet enough so he only had to push the pipe through it, and large chunks would drop to the floor. Behind it, batts of insulation drooped out, once yellow, now black with water stains and mold. A large chunk pulled away and hit the floor with a wet slap.

Cady kept clearing insulation and sheetrock, trying to make the hole as wide as possible. The floor supports were set a little more than a foot apart. He was sure he could pass between them. Judging by where the stairway was, he'd come up through the floor of the study, underneath the water-damaged window. The green sofa, probably angled outward to keep its feet off the weakened floorboards, would shield him from Fritch, who should be passed out in his chair. If he woke, maybe he'd think Cady was a hallucination.

Around him, things chittered and clattered in the dark. He imagined a thick blanket of centipedes covering the floor. As long as they kept to the shadows, he paid them no mind.

Often, he caught himself looking at the glass of pink on the floor of his cell. Each look brought a wave of relief that it hadn't been knocked over, followed by a debate about whether he should knock it over himself. As dangerous as it was, he decided he'd better keep it around for emergencies.

Between the floor supports, a layer of plywood was visible. It was black and soft and yielded readily to the end of his pipe. Closer to the wall, the wood gave so easily he needed only to rub the pipe against it to make slivers and splinters fall free.

Muscle cramps ripped through his right hand, re-aggravated injuries from when he'd taken his cell apart, and once they got so bad he dropped the pipe. He went for a sip of pink then but found dust and bits of mold and wood floating in it. Trying to fish them out with his finger made it worse. With a sigh, he gave up and poured the glass through the bars. His heart sank as the pink splashed on the floor. So far, the full glass outside looked uncontaminated. He pushed it further away, hoping to keep it clean. Just in case he needed it later.

Having never built a house, Cady had no idea how many layers of wood he'd have to gouge his way through to get free, but as the plywood came away, it revealed the slats of floorboards, old, warped, and discolored with water damage of their own.

He could almost feel the rain on his skin already.

15

The first centipede didn't show up until he pushed
a floorboard with his pipe. It lifted with a little more
effort than Cady expected, but as soon as the crack between it and the next board widened, the centipede
dropped through. It landed across the back of his hand,
scampered up his arm, and wrapped itself around his
neck like a scarf.

The pipe clanged off the metal bed frame and clattered to the floor while Cady fell on his ass. He scrubbed
at his neck, trying to kill the thing, but he couldn't find it.

A drilling pain in his left arm helped him refocus.
A rusty nail had pierced his forearm when he'd landed
in the pile of rubble. It hadn't gone deep, but it took Cady
a moment to work up the nerve to yank it free.

The nail squirmed in his hand; he caught a glimpse

of buggy little eyes looking at him, and he threw it at the wall with a yell. It pinged off the stone and landed with an arched roll before coming to a stop, a nail again.

Cady stood. He refused to use the bars for leverage, in defiance of the pink and his pain.

Something moved outside his cell. He tried not to look but couldn't help it. The pipes in the workroom had transformed into centipedes, every damn one. They scratched and rolled over each other, silvery and squiggling, eyes, legs, and carapaces roiling in a pile while their antennae batted everything in sight.

Cady heard a low moan. Knew it was his own.

He reached for his pipe and froze mid-bend. *Now* the thing had segments on it. He closed his eyes. Steeled his nerve. Told himself again and again this was nothing more than the effect of the pink, showing him horrible things, making him crazy.

The pipe was a pipe again.

Cady snatched it up and turned his attention back to the ceiling.

Once he cleared away enough of the floorboards, he'd have to reach up through and pull himself between the support beams. Shouldn't be a problem.

He pushed up on a different floorboard with the pipe. It didn't move. The wood seemed a little spongy, but nothing like the plywood had been. Cady used the pipe to test a few more floorboards, found most of them had *some* give to them.

So far, everything he'd accomplished had caused very little revealing noise. His luck had run out, however.

To get through this last layer, he was going to have to hammer at the wood.

This was when he should pray. Cady remembered the night he'd walked away from Alcoholics Anonymous. The night he'd tested their boundaries and found them to be serious about turning their lives over to God. They used a watered-down cop-out, "God as we understand him," but it was still pledging servitude to an imaginary being. Cady had believed then as he believed now. There was no magical being supervising humankind, itching to avail Its magnificence on those who asked.

Cady was alone.

He looked over his shoulder, saw the silvery centipedes inching their way closer to his cell. Soon enough, they would be inside with him, scurrying up his legs.

He hoped Fritch had taken enough pink to knock him out. He didn't need the man stomping him back down into the hole as he was trying to climb out.

No sense worrying until he got these boards free.

He gripped the pipe. Aimed.

"Cady."

Cady dropped the pole again, spun and pressed himself against the wall. Poonchuck stood just outside the bars.

But it wasn't Poonchuck. Not really. Within the red mess where his nose had been, an insectile face stared at him. Its antennae were pulled back smooth to the man's skull, like a demonic comb-over. Along his arms and legs, millions of pointy little feet kicked, making his clothes billow.

Cady swallowed his screams. He looked down, saw Poonchuck lying on the floor in the same position.

In front of him, the other Poonchuck took a step forward and bumped into the bars.

"You're not real," Cady said.

The centipede face within the bullet hole turned slightly, as if cocking its head. It pressed against the bars, and fragments of the man's shirt pulled away in the shape of segments and legs, crawled around the bars into the cell, and re-formed back into shirt again. It moved slowly, more and more of it passing like a million creatures melded into one being, entering the cell around the bars, one leggy section at a time.

Cady loosed the scream building in his throat. He scooped the pipe from the floor, keeping his eyes on the advancing creature, and came up swinging. Each strike passed through Poonchuck's body as the centipedes parted, letting the pipe clang off the cell bars.

"Cady."

He panicked. Cady grabbed the bed frame, still on its side, and thrust it across the cell to crash in the corner under the hole. He took two quick steps and leaped up onto the side rail, crunching his knee on the metal while his sore hands and his face slapped against the stone wall.

A moment of dizziness. Cady looked back over his shoulder, took a deep breath when he only saw the real Poonchuck, bloody and dead on the floor.

He inhaled deeply to calm himself, then saw the wriggly, out-of-focus Poonchuck standing beside the footboard of his cot. His hands rested on the metal, antennae pulsing in the air from the tips of each finger.

With a shout, Cady hammered the heel of his hand against the floorboards over his head. He must have dropped the pipe when he'd jumped.

His first strike lifted a board a full inch with the panicked screech of a nail pulling free. His wrist bent too far backward, so he switched to his fist. He pounded at the board again, and it popped up completely. Then he started on the one next to it.

Glances into his cell revealed slow progress as the centipede Poonchuck tried to climb the bed the same way it had come through the bars, one leggy fragment at a time. He heard scuffling further away, imagined a centipede-Trilling in the next room, filthy with grave dirt, crawling along the hall.

Cady focused on his job. Three boards came away. Four.

From above, Fritch's voice. "Belle?"

Cady grabbed another floorboard, shoved. It seemed further away from him than the others had. The bed rail was giving way under his weight.

Another panicked flurry sent two floorboards aside.

Now or never, he thought.

He reached through the hole and caught the support beam. As soon as he lifted his feet, he realized that if his grip slipped, he would land straddling the side rail of the bed. At the last possible second, his feet found purchase on the wall, and he used it for leverage, kicking himself upward while pulling his weight through the hole.

He kicked hard and managed to get his head through, one arm to either side of him.

The back of the green couch stood like an angled fabric wall to his left. The warped study window hung just over him, right where he'd thought it would be.

Cady kicked and grabbed the sill with his right hand. The board wobbled a bit, but it held while he pulled up hard, kicked his legs some more, and managed to work his left leg up out of the hole.

"Elise? Izzat you?"

Water ran down his face as he worked his right leg free. He thought it was the rain, wondered why it was warm, wondered why it was falling inside the house.

He was crying.

He got his right knee on the floor and collapsed sideways, panting and staring up at the maroon curtains. He had a vague memory of thinking they were ugly the first time he'd seen them. Now, though, they were the most beautiful things he'd ever seen in his life.

"Elise, you're not supposed to be here."

Fritch was only a few feet away.

Cady pulled himself into a sitting position.

Something popped. A fire. Fritch must have one blazing in the fireplace.

Cady found his feet and stood, using the green couch to support his weight. The fabric seemed to be kicking at him, trying to buck him off.

"You're not Elise," Fritch said.

Cady gasped at the sight of Fritch's chitinous face watching him from the recliner across the room. Antennae rose from his forehead in the shape of a "V." An instant later, he realized the man's very human hand held the gun.

"Get back where you came from," Fritch said.

On the table beside Fritch stood an empty pitcher next to a half-full glass of pink. On top of a full glass in the cellar, Fritch should be about ready to pass out.

"I came to warn you," Cady said. "Elise is coming in here any minute."

"Liar," the man said. His wrist bucked, and the gun fired. Cady hollered and jerked away, almost dropping back into the hole by accident. The bullet, though, punched into the wall to his right.

"You don't speak the name of my wife. You aren't man enough to speak the name of my wife."

Cady decided to inch his way along the couch toward the fireplace. Behind Fritch, the wall of books started to come undone as each spine grew hundreds of kicking legs.

Fritch swung the gun toward him. Cady dove forward, rolling over the back of the couch just as the shot blasted over him.

"What did you do to Elise?" Fritch yelled.

The gun fired again as Cady rolled off the couch. He shoved the coffee table up on its side, spilling magazines and empty glasses on the floor at Fritch's feet.

Through the glass tabletop, Fritch pointed the gun at Cady's face.

Click.

Fritch looked at the gun. To Cady, it seemed to be

clinging to Fritch's hand by itself, hugging his fingers with bony legs. The barrel hole sprouted antennae, two eyes.

Fritch thrust himself forward in his chair.

Cady scrambled up from the floor. The big man had no doubt decided to beat him to death. Cady eyed the fireplace tools on his side of the hearth, ignored the way their segments vacillated. Fritch reached for him but tripped over the upturned coffee table.

Cady leaped backward, grabbed the fireplace poker, and held it before him like a sword. The pointed end snapped around and chattered at him, antennae springing from its head as it darted toward him, mouth wide like a snake. He screamed and dropped it.

Fritch came off the couch quickly, more quickly than Cady would've thought possible, charging at him like a battering ram, hands out in front.

In desperation, Cady side-stepped, put his hands on the man's back and shoved down, propelling him head first through the glass front of the fireplace.

The screaming was instantaneous. Fritch's feet flailed a bit before finding purchase and pulling him out of the inferno. He came away with his head and hands on fire, the flames eating his shirt, burning legs and antennae frantic about him.

Fritch leaped to his feet and ran, slammed into the leather recliner, then collapsed to the floor.

"DAD!"

Ezzy stood in the study doorway, her face a mask of terror and fury. She ripped off her coat and smothered Fritch's head and arms, screaming the whole time.

Cady couldn't look away. Ezzy had called him "Dad."

Poonchuck said Fritch's daughter was the mastermind behind all this. But Poonchuck was mean. He'd say anything to get what he wanted. Ezzy *couldn't* be involved, no matter *how* much her segmented hair writhed on her head.

Cady noted the rug, the recliner, and some of the magazines from the coffee table were aflame. This house was very old, he remembered. Ezzy had grown up here. Its wood would be dry, ready to burn. Even as he contemplated this, the siding on the wall behind the bar caught. Smoke rose to fill the upper part of the room. On the shelves, leggy books kicked and wrestled, trying to escape.

Ezzy had a gun pointed at him. That couldn't be—

Click.

"Oh," Cady said.

She'd found Fritch's gun on the floor. Tried to kill him. She was not his girlfriend; she was not in danger. She, in fact, *was* the danger.

He couldn't get past her to the door. She had too many legs, too many claws to grab him. Her midsection bent, curled even as segments grew, stretching her, making her longer, more formidable.

The flames spread. Fritch twitched weakly. Cady raised a hand to ward off Ezzy's evil stare, thinking he would turn to stone, thinking she'd become a Gorgon with centipedes for hair instead of snakes.

He stared at his arm. Bony legs jutted out from each side. Antennae batted the air from his own fingertips.

Cady screamed and scrambled over the green couch. If he couldn't get to the door, he'd open the window.

He landed inches from the hole. He imagined what would've happened if he'd hit it dead on. Falling in again, no hope of escape.

Ezzy came around the couch, flinging the standing lamp aside. The cord either broke or pulled from the wall, killing the light. Everything danced in the fire's orange fury. Ezzy drew back a fist, then disappeared.

Her screech made Cady clap his hands over his ears.

Cady didn't know what happened. Then he saw her, one leg jammed into the hole, the other twisted awkwardly behind her. She screamed and clawed at the windowsill, insectile legs poking out of her fingers.

He looked at his own hands. Saw nothing buggy about them. Rolled back over the couch once more, back into the smoke. He shoved the couch against the wall as hard as he could. Ezzy screamed behind it. He grabbed the legs of the coffee table and wedged them beneath the front.

The study burned. The smoke filled his lungs. Every cough felt like centipedes were trapped in his throat, knotted in a ball and wrestling to free themselves. The urge to dart in and out of the bar to score some pink nearly overwhelmed him. He was sure he could succeed before succumbing to the flames.

Fritch had stopped moving. His body was completely engulfed. The line of legs along his side burned like twigs. The doorframe leading to the foyer danced with fire. Even the end of the couch nearest the fireplace was burning now. The heat was immense.

One option remained.

He grabbed the fireplace poker from the floor and nearly dropped it again it was so hot. Tolerating it, he smashed it through the window glass over the couch. Ezzy screamed as shards landed on her.

He climbed the couch, ducked through the window, and dove for freedom. If there were centipedes out here, they kept their distance and let him hit the ground hard.

CADY, NOW

16

The numbing blanket of unconsciousness began to unravel. Cady scrunched his eyes as raindrops pelted his face. Something in the study popped. A shard of hot glass landed on his arm, spurring him into motion.

He made it to his feet, but the world teetered like a ship in a storm. The light from the burning house bounced and flickered. Centipedes thrashed on the lawn.

Ezzy screamed. He scrambled to his feet and ran from the sound. Things squished beneath his sneakers. Something tried to wrap itself around his ankle. He shrieked and kicked it away. They would swarm him if he stopped.

He aimed for the long driveway, thinking he could make the street and get help, but already the sound of sirens split the air. The house wasn't as far removed from civilization as he'd been told.

He did not want to be around for questioning when the authorities showed up. Cady turned and bolted for the woods at the edge of the property. Centipedes would be teeming in there, masked beneath the shadows, waiting to drop on his head from the trees. Still, he preferred his chances in there. Whatever was coming to douse the flames might be an army of people-bugs. He wanted no more to do with them.

He ducked behind a thick tree. Waited. Listened.

Things moved at his feet. Brush rustled. *Squirrels,* he told himself.

The front door of the house crashed open, and a body fell out. It swam in flames, collapsed face-first down the two steps to the ground. Fire crawled off the body, nibbling first, and then taking stubborn bites of the lawn.

The body was too small to be Fritch, too short to be Poonchuck. It must be Ezzy. She must have pulled herself up even though her leg had bent the wrong way. How had she made it to the door?

Bright flashing lights screamed into view. Bodies covered in black shadows leaped out of the truck even before it stopped. If these people caught him, they'd put him in a cell again. Trap him with his fears. Keep him high until he killed himself.

They'd never find him. He hoped not, anyway. He couldn't move anymore. The numbness was wrapping around him again. It would not be denied.

Cady lowered himself to the ground. If the centipedes wanted him, nothing could stop them now. His head hit the dirt, his vision faded, and the pink pulled him under as the trees leaned over him, their branches kicking and grabbing at him.

ABOUT THE AUTHOR

Paul McMahon has been writing since his Junior year in high school, when he won an argument with his English teacher by writing his first story in second-person narrative. He is a current member of the New England Horror Writers, and has appeared in every NEHW anthology to date, including WICKED TALES, WICKED WITCHES, and WICKED HAUNTED. He's also been published in the anthologies FLESH LIKE SMOKE and CAPED. This is his first novel.

CHAPTER ONE

It was one of those rare mornings when Dennis Parkes woke at peace. Cautiously, he lifted his head, waiting for the quick, shadowy movements seen from the corner of his eye, the sibilant whispering filling the stale air of the small bedroom. There was nothing. Just still, silent darkness.

He thought of waking his wife, Swan, to share his sense of relief and happiness, but she had never heard the voices or seen the shadows move. If he woke her, she would be angry at being disturbed more than an hour before the alarm was due. It would ruin his mood. It would ruin the stillness. He eased his head back onto the pillow and lay awake, enjoying the silence, the peace.

Slowly, dawn lit up the window through the thin curtains, and birdsong twittered and whistled through the trees of nearby Ottmor Wood. If only all mornings could be like this, he would not need the medication, the therapy. It might even make his life with Swan less combative.

If only.

Wyatt Road lay quiet and sleepy on the outskirts of Anbal, a small village on the Wirral Peninsula. The commuter traffic, from Liverpool to the north and Chester to the south, bypassed Anbal on the M53 motorway. What little diverted through the narrow main street of the village itself passed the end of Wyatt Road without any thought of turning in. Wyatt Road was a dead-end. If you didn't live there and were not visiting, your only destination would be the turning circle just before the wooden stile leading to Ottmor Wood.

It was the quiet, more than anything, that had drawn Swanhild Parkes to number 20 when it came up for sale. A narrow mid-terraced house, it stood more or less equidistant between the end of the road and the wood. Built in the early 1930s, it had more-recent additions of a concrete driveway at the front, newly installed plumbing and electrics, and a narrow, but long, well-groomed garden at the back. That was eleven years ago, when she had persuaded Dennis that this should be their first family home. Now, standing at the kitchen sink, staring at the overgrown lawn, the legs of upturned plastic chairs like skeletal limbs reaching up from the long grass, she felt nothing but despair.

"It's not my fault I got made redundant," shouted

Dennis from somewhere behind her. She had almost forgotten they were mid-argument. The same argument they had had almost weekly for the last three years.

"No," she said, agreeing. "But it is your fault that the grass hasn't been cut for weeks."

"You know it hurts my back."

"We can't afford to get someone in anymore," she said, striving to be both truthful and understanding. "Since you can't do it, *I'll* have to do it at the weekend."

"I'll worry if you do that. I don't want you to do that."

His voice almost whined. She hated it when he whined.

"Yes, well, there's not much choice, is there?" She turned from the sink to face her husband. "Now, I have to get to work."

"I'll move the car," said Dennis. "May as well go to the shop while I'm out."

He turned and began burrowing through the accumulated clutter under the stairs for his shoes.

Swan wanted to be even more truthful. She wanted to tell her husband that he was a morbidly obese, out-of-work man in his early forties, and that it was no wonder his back and joints hurt, given the weight they were carrying. But she knew the redundancy had hurt him badly, destroyed his confidence, shoved him into depression, and that the weight gain was almost completely due to emotional eating since then. He was not currently fit for work, mentally or physically. She wanted to tell him these things, but she knew it would just deepen his depression and worsen an already terrible self-image. He needed to know she supported him, still loved him, despite all that had happened.

Dennis had found his shoes and, with some difficulty, put them on. Breathing heavily, he led the way out of the front door. Swan shrugged on her one and only coat and followed.

Dennis reversed his old Peugeot 405 out of the narrow driveway and waited, the engine idling. He felt comfortable in the car, able to relax, away from whispered voices, away from Swan. Alone. It had been bought for the long drive to his last place of work, and he held on to it stubbornly after the redundancy. Big and impractical it might be, given how little driving he now did, but it was *his*. And it was the only thing that connected him to his old life. His purposeful, *employed* life. When he hadn't felt quite so worthless. When he didn't spend days in introspection and deepening depresssion. When he felt confident his wife loved him.

Swan's Vauxhall Corsa reversed out, and the bright pink of the bodywork pulled a slight smile out of his frown. Even she agreed she bought it more for the colour than the car itself.

They waved to each other as she drove off, and Dennis waited until he saw her safely negotiate the junction at the end of the road before he put the Peugeot into gear and headed for the shops.

Just get the essentials and back home.

But did he really want to be home? There was nothing there but an empty house, another long day of watching the clock ticking slowly by, the flash of movement from the corner of his eye—and the voices.

He wanted to tell Swan, he really did. But how do you tell your wife that you hear voices in the home you share? She already thought him fat and useless, blamed him for his depression and for failing to get another job. To admit to hearing voices and seeing things would finally convince her he was completely insane. She would probably leave. He couldn't risk that.

Only two other people knew about the voices and the shadows: his local general practitioner, Dr. Banks, and his one and only friend, Travis Newman. The only two people he had told differed in their reactions.

"It's not that unusual," Dr. Banks had said. "Particularly in someone suffering from clinical depression, like yourself."

"But what do the voices mean?" said Dennis. "Why are they mostly unintelligible? Shouldn't they be sending me messages from God or something?"

Dr. Banks smiled. "The mind is a complex thing," he said. "It can push bad and unpleasant thoughts aside if it doesn't want to deal with them. It separates them, and they become a different part of you."

"You mean like another person in my head?"

"Not quite, but another aspect of you, certainly." Dr. Banks removed his narrow-framed glasses and held them in his right hand, twisting them back and forth as he spoke. "These are things you don't want to have to cope with just now, so they're pushed into the background. And mostly, that's where they stay. But every now and then they push back, and that's where the voices are coming from."

"So it's all in my mind," said Dennis. "Does this mean I'm psychotic or something?"

Dr. Banks shook his head. "No. It's not any kind of psychosis. It's *dissociation*. Like I said, it's quite common among those suffering from depression."

Travis, on the other hand, saw things slightly differently.

"So, you hear voices. Are they always in your head, or sometimes from outside?"

They had been sitting in their local Sainsburys cafe, meeting up during Travis's lunch break from his nearby office job, and before Dennis went shopping. Talking with Travis boosted Dennis's self-confidence enough to make it round the aisles without panicking.

"Sometimes in my head, sometimes not," said Dennis, keeping his voice low. He was sure some of the old people at neighbouring tables were listening.

"I don't reckon it's anything to do with depression," said Travis, casually dismissing what Dennis had told him about the doctor's opinion. "I think it's a lot simpler than all that stuff."

"Oh yes?" said Dennis, doubtfully. As a general rule, he sided with doctors over laymen, but he always had time for Travis's thoughts on matters, however outrageous they might turn out to be. "And so what do you think it is?"

"Simple." Travis leaned closer, lowering his voice to a whisper. "Your house is *haunted*."

Weekend Getaway

Bram Stoker Award winning author
TOM DEADY

with an Introduction by
Josh Malerman

CHAPTER ONE

Now

I tightened the noose around my neck, then yanked it off with a grunt. I had referred to neckties as nooses for as long as I could remember; anyone that had to wear one every day to work was slowly killing themselves. And here was I, like an old fool, trying to attach one to my own neck.

With a tired sigh, I tried again to make the knot. Finally, Mary came over and pushed my hands to my sides, and with a few deft movements, had it looking perfect.

"There you go, Dad." She smiled and gave me a hug. "Mom always loved you in a tie, so you have to look nice for her this one last time." If there was ever an occasion that a tie was perfect for, it was a funeral.

She broke down then, after being my rock through

the whole mess. I held her close while my own tears spilled. I was sure I'd be out of them by now, but they just kept coming. When she pulled away, her face held a determined smile.

"We should go. There'll be plenty of time for this later."

She was my rock again. I nodded, silently chastising myself. *I should be the strong one. She just lost her mother.*

* * *

The service was lovely, as funerals go. My wife was one of the good ones. After the priest said his final words at the grave, I remained there alone, shooing anyone away, including Mary, who tried to talk to me, to console me. I stared at the opening in the ground, wanting nothing more than to crawl in with my wife and let them cover me with dirt. I don't know how long I stayed like that, the never-ending tears dripping down my face, absently rubbing my ghost finger. *God, what I'd give for another day with her.*

Finally, I trudged back to the car. Everybody would be back at the house, eating and drinking and talking like nothing had happened. I hated the tradition. I just wanted to be alone. To think, or *not* to think, and to wonder why I wasn't the one to go first.

I drove home, listening to an oldies station, taking my time. The day was overcast—as if the sun didn't want to attend such a sad event—the sky heavy with rain. A perfect day for a funeral. I would have preferred pouring rain and gusting wind. An angry day, to match my mood.

The scene at the house was just what I expected. A lot of people laughing, everybody eating and holding either a beer or a glass of wine. A fucking party, minus one guest. I played my part as best I could, making the rounds, accepting condolences, sharing memories, always a glass of water in my hand. *Maybe just one drink today, something to take the edge off.* I stuck with water, though, as it wasn't a day to get sloppy.

As the afternoon wore on, people began drifting away. I guess they thought they'd put in the appropriate time and wanted to get back to their lives. Most of them I wouldn't see until the next death. I looked around at the mess, too overwhelmed to even think about cleaning. Instead, I tossed a dirty napkin on the coffee table and plopped onto the couch.

It was just Mary and her husband, Jeff, and their son, Nick. Jeff was a good guy, some sort of computer programmer. He made good money, but more im-portantly, treated my Mary like a queen. *What more could a dad ask for?*

Little Nick looked just like his dad; tall and thin for his age with a face that looked wise beyond his seven years. Mary started picking up in the kitchen, but I waved her off. "Leave it. Come sit with me for a while, I'm too tired to even watch you clean."

They spread out on the couches and chairs around me. Empty cups and bottles littered the room, along with half-empty plates of funeral food. I pushed some trash aside to make room for my water glass. I was with my family, what was left of it, anyway. We talked a while about the service, and a little while longer about some of the folks we hadn't seen in a while. Nick was getting antsy. It was a long day of being good for him, for any kid his age.

He climbed onto my lap and looked up at me. His eyes were so full of wonder and curiosity, so full of youth that it made my heart yearn for such innocence. I wondered when my own eyes had lost that. *You know when.* His little hand clasped my gnarled old-man hand and pulled it to his face. "Grampy, you never told me the story of how you lost your finger."

Lake Livingston: August, 1961

Mark Gaitlin is 15, the son of one of the wealthiest men in Texas, and on the most boring summer vacation of his life. His days are filled with the pomp and circumstance of country club life, while his nights are a parade of one embarrassment after another at the hands of giggling teenage girls.

But the piney woods above Lake Livingston are dark at night, and they hold many secrets for an impressionable youngster on the cusp of becoming a man. And one night, after skinny dipping in the lake with a mysterious local girl, Mark Gaitlin's life takes a crazy turn into the fire and brimstone religion of backwoods snake handlers and abandoned villages haunted by old family secrets. If he can survive the snakes and the ghosts and his own family's dark history, he just might make it out of the woods alive.

And something else…he just might become a man.

Death awaits you. Tim Ritter has just a few months left. At least that's what the doctors have told him.

But then he's been offered a second chance at life – and love. For a price. But is the price too high? The sacrifice too great?

Find out one man's answer to those questions in Dan Foley's Gypsy, now available in print and for Kindle, Nook, and Kobo e-readers.